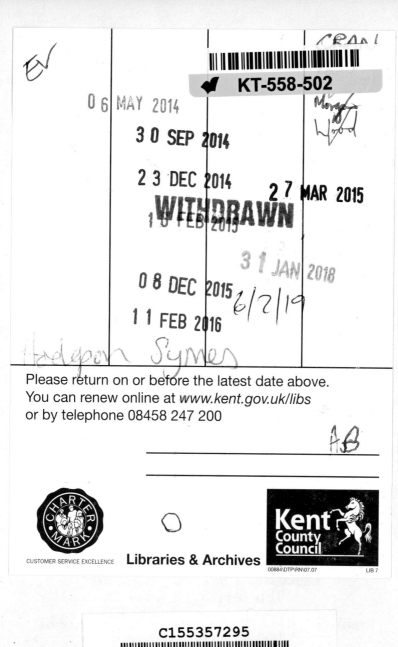

MISS PETERSON
& THE COLONEL

Lydia Peterson is content to run her stud farm and remain single — she doesn't want the autocratic Colonel Simon Wescott interfering with her life. However, thrown together by a series of dramatic events, their lives become endangered, forcing them to reconsider their first impressions. Will Simon be able to compromise his duty to put King and country first, in order to save Lydia's life? Can she give up her independence and become a soldier's wife?

Books by Fenella Miller
in the Linford Romance Library:

THE RETURN OF LORD RIVENHALL
A COUNTRY MOUSE
A RELUCTANT BRIDE
A DANGEROUS DECEPTION
MISTAKEN IDENTITY
LORD ATHERTON'S WARD
LADY CHARLOTTE'S SECRET
CHRISTMAS AT HARTFORD HALL
MISS SHAW & THE DOCTOR
TO LOVE AGAIN
MISS BANNERMAN AND THE DUKE

FENELLA MILLER

MISS PETERSON & THE COLONEL

Complete and Unabridged

LINFORD
Leicester

First published in Great Britain in 2012

First Linford Edition
published 2013

British Library CIP Data

Miller, Fenella-Jane.
  Miss Peterson & the Colonel.- -
(Linford romance library)
  1. Love stories.
  2. Large type books.
  I. Title II. Series
  823.9'2–dc23

  ISBN 978–1–4448–1505–4

Published by
F. A. Thorpe (Publishing)
Anstey, Leicestershire

Set by Words & Graphics Ltd.
Anstey, Leicestershire
Printed and bound in Great Britain by
T. J. International Ltd., Padstow, Cornwall

This book is printed on acid-free paper

'You Cannot Abandon Us'

Lydia grabbed at the strap as the carriage tilted but failed to stop her undignified slide into the well. Her maid landed heavily on top of her. For a moment she lay winded, unable to move.

'I beg your pardon, miss, I couldn't stop myself from falling.'

'It's not your fault, Martha. I think we must have broken an axle. I sincerely hope the horses are un-harmed.' With some difficulty she extricated herself and stood up. 'At least we are both in one piece. If I balance on the edge of the seat I believe I might manage to open the door.' She attempted the manoeuvre and the coach rocked alarmingly.

'Please don't do that, Miss Peterson. You'll likely have us right over.'

'Why doesn't Jim come to our aid?

1

Do you think he's taken a tumble from the box. As Billy has gone ahead to order our refreshments he cannot assist. I must get out.'

This time her struggles sent the coach crashing right over. Her world turned upside down, her legs and arms became entangled with Martha's and it was several minutes before she was able to get both of them upright.

Martha screamed and pointed down. Lydia saw water seeping in through the door that now acted as the floor. They must have turned over into the ditch that ran alongside the road.

'Hold on to something, Martha. I think if I could step on your knee I might reach the door handle somehow.'

Her smart travelling ensemble was ruined, the hem already saturated with muddy water and her spencer in no better case. Her lovely new bonnet was hanging in disarray around her neck. Her sister had been most insistent she dressed in her best to meet the colonel, as the much longed for visitor was to arrive today as well. She was not going to impress anyone now.

The whinnying and stamping from the team had stopped. Was this a good or bad sign? Before she had time to consider, the door above her head was slammed back and a gentleman appeared in the space. His features were indistinct, but from his voice he was obviously well-to-do.

'Why couldn't you stay still, ladies? You have turned a minor accident into a major disaster. I have released your horses and attended to your coachman, however now that you've managed to tip the carriage over there is nothing I can do to get you out without assistance. You must stay inside.'

The incredibly rude gentleman vanished as suddenly as he'd appeared.

'Come back here this instant, sir. You cannot abandon us in here.'

He slammed his fist against the carriage and shouted back. 'I cannot right the vehicle unaided, and can't pull you out through the door. You will come to no harm, the ditch is shallow, I shall be back as soon as I can.'

Then he was gone, only the sound of hoofbeats echoing in the cold winter air to keep her company. This was no gentleman. He had callously left her and Martha without making a serious attempt to rescue them. He could be gone for hours. What about poor Jim possibly unconscious on the side of the road?

She would not remain incarcerated a moment longer.

'Martha, let me stand on your knee. If you brace yourself against the seat I'm certain I can scramble out.'

With her maid as a stool, she grasped the edges of the open door. 'Martha, give me a push.'

Her feet were grasped firmly and she rose steadily. Throwing herself forward, she tipped headlong through the door and slithered, skirts and petticoats flying, down the side to land with a thud in the road.

'I'm out, Martha. I shall come back

to you in a moment. I must check on Jim and the horses first.'

Three of the team were standing dejectedly in the shelter of the hedge that bordered the lane. There was no sign of Jim and the fourth horse. Good grief! The wretched man had used the lead horse to convey her coachman. Surely it would have been better to wait until a cart could be brought round?

She must get Martha out and her precious chestnuts to shelter. The White Queen could be no more than two miles away; that must be where her would-be rescuer had gone for help.

'Martha, if I lower the reins to you, you must take hold of them. I shall attach the other end to one of the horses. I think it will be possible to pull you out.'

'I shall do my best, miss, but I'm a fair weight. I reckon they might not hold.'

With ingenuity and the help of Rufus, the most amenable of the remaining three horses, Martha emerged through the door a short while later.

'We're only a brief ride from the hostelry. If I lead you do you think you could stay on board Rufus for that short distance?'

Martha viewed the animal with disfavour but nodded. 'I reckon even riding that beast is better than standing around here getting frozen to the marrow.'

Less than half an hour later, Lydia arrived at her destination, leading one horse with her maid upon it and the spare horse following behind. Her side-saddle had been stored under the box and she'd managed to remove it.

Martha scrambled down. 'If you don't mind, I shall remain here, Miss Peterson, until someone comes for me.'

Two ostlers ran forward to take the horses and Lydia gave them coins from her reticule. Turning to her maid, she smiled sympathetically.

'Here, take my purse. There's more than enough to pay for a private parlour and a chamber. I'm going to ride the remaining distance to London and fetch assistance. It's no more than five miles, it won't take me too long.'

Lydia had no intention of setting off unaccompanied and was relieved to see her errant groom who had gone ahead to order refreshments, hurrying across to greet her.

'Billy, is Jim badly hurt?'

'He's broken his arm and had a knock on the head, but he's been attended to.'

'And that obnoxious gentleman, is he here?'

'The gentleman ain't, miss. He set off a few minutes ago with half a dozen men to right the carriage and rescue you. He left from the lane at the back otherwise you would have seen him.'

Her abigail was bound to see to Jim. This meant she was free to leave. The irascible gentleman would not be pleased she had already left the scene of the accident.

'Saddle Pegasus and then we can leave immediately. Lady Grayson is expecting me. Lord Grayson will no doubt arrange to collect Martha, Jim and the baggage.'

In less than an hour she cantered through the archway and into the stable yard at the back of her sister's smart townhouse. She was sadly dishevelled, but there was nothing she could do about it. Leaving Billy to attend to the horses, she hurried in through a side door. Ellen would understand and allow her to remain away from Colonel Wescott until her trunks arrived.

Using the back stairs, she hurried to the apartment she always used. Fortunately she kept several changes of clothing here so she could remove her ruined garments before explaining to her sister and brother-in-law what had transpired. Seeing her in such disarray might upset Ellen and that would not do so late in the pregnancy.

Edward, Lord Grayson, found the whole tale amusing and immediately sent his carriage to rescue Martha and Sam.

'Reynolds, my man of business, will take care of everything for you, my dear. Rest assured, your vehicle will be restored to you in pristine condition before you return to Bracken Hall.'

Ellen was less easily placated. 'Lydia, why is it that disaster follows in your wake? Please promise me you will not become embroiled in any further such happenings during your visit? I do so wish you and dear Simon to be friends.'

'Where is he? I thought he would be here today.'

'He has been delayed. He will not reach us until this evening. You can wait until tomorrow to be introduced, my dear. After so much excitement I'm sure you will wish to eat in your room tonight.' Ellen tilted her cheek for a kiss.

'I have never been sanguine about Edward allowing you to live as you please. He is your guardian after all.'

'And an excellent one he is, too.

9

David will reach his majority in the summer and be able to take over.'

Her sister laughed. 'Poppycock, my love. The poor boy will continue to do as you bid.' Ellen raised a hand to prevent Lydia's denial. 'I know you pretend to follow his wishes on the small points, but we both know it is you that holds the reins.'

'As long as both he and Edward are content then why should I wish to change things?'

'Run along, my love. It would not do to be seen as you are. I warn you, Simon is not so easily disarmed. He is a man used to command. Indeed, he can be quite fierce sometimes.'

'Then I shall not like him. If he is not kind to you.'

'Good heavens, you have got me wrong. Simon is a dear boy, a perfect gentleman. I was referring to his dealing with his men. Edward has told me much about it.'

'Then I shall make my own mind up when we meet. No, do not get up. I shall see myself out.' She stooped to kiss her sister and hurried to the rooms she always used on her visits to town.

The last thing she wanted was to meet this hero of Waterloo dressed as she was. Although it might be the sensible thing to do, in her outmoded gown he would no doubt take one look at her and decide she was a dowd. She might not wish to marry him, but did not intend to give him reason to take her in dislike.

She was certain both Ellen and Edward wanted them to make a match of it, but she had no plans to give up her independence to a soldier, indeed, to any man. She had her stud farm to run with her brother, David, and no man could ever equal the love she had for her horses.

★ ★ ★

The next morning she dressed quickly and hurried down, hoping to slip outside and see for herself that her chestnuts were none the worse for their adventure.

Foster, the elderly butler, greeted her politely. 'I trust you have recovered from your eventful journey, Miss Peterson. Lord Grayson is in the drawing-room. He requests that you join him at your convenience.'

'Thank you, Foster. How is your rheumatism this winter? I expect the cold weather has been plaguing you.'

The grey-haired gentleman almost smiled. 'I've not been too bad, Miss Peterson. The damp and cold sets it off but thankfully we have had a relatively dry winter.'

Lydia paused to admire the spacious entrance hall, as always warm and welcoming, the chequered floor immaculate, the grand staircase freshly waxed and not a cobweb in sight. She wished she could say the same about Bracken Hall. Her interests lay outside the house and her housekeeper Dorcas, bless her, was a trifle short-sighted.

No doubt Edward wished to tell her

what had transpired after she'd left The White Queen yesterday. She hurried toward the drawing-room, halting in the doorway. Edward was not alone; another gentleman stood beside him and they were deep in conversation.

Colonel Wescott had risen far earlier than one might have expected. She took this opportunity to study him unobserved. He was unmistakably Edward's brother, but where the older man's features were soft everything about the colonel was the opposite. He was a head taller and his shoulders broader, but his face intrigued her. His skin was tanned, his teeth a flash of white as he spoke. His nose was sharp, uncompromising, his eyebrows a slash of black above his deep set eyes.

She coughed politely and they turned to stare at her. Their reaction could not have been more different. Edward advanced, smiling, to greet her. His brother stiffened and then raked her with a glance which obviously found her wanting.

'My dear girl, see who is here. You will not believe what I have to tell you.'

Lydia flushed. Something about Colonel Wescott was horribly familiar.

'Come, let me introduce you to my brother.' Edward's tone was bland, but his eyes were brimming with amusement. 'I rather think you two have already met.'

Reluctantly, she turned to the formidable gentleman. Keeping her eyes lowered, she curtsied, glancing through her lashes as she did so. He bowed but he was quite definitely glowering at her. Despite her trepidation, she noticed his eyes were an unusual shade, the blue so dark as to be almost black.

'I'm delighted to meet you again, Miss Peterson. I would have been even more delighted if you had remained in your carriage as instructed and not sent me on a fool's errand yesterday.'

'You, sir, were most unpleasant. I had no idea who you were, and felt it necessary to ride at once to the home of my sister.' She gave him glare for glare. 'The fact that I, a mere female, was able to get myself and my maid out safely indicates that you deliberately left us where we were in order to punish us for tipping the carriage over.'

For a moment the matter hung in the balance, then the colonel bowed and she thought she saw a flicker of admiration in his eyes. Thinking it best to change the subject, she forced her lips into a smile and said the first thing that came into her head.

'I believe you to be the first hero of the Peninsula I have met. It must be a great relief to you that Bonaparte is safely captured.'

He raised an eyebrow as if surprised. 'Exactly so. It is to be hoped that he remains on Elba. The country has been at war for too many years.'

There was an awkward pause. Why didn't Edward step in with some commonplace remark? Then she realised her brother-in-law had wandered to the far end of the room, leaving her alone to smooth things over with this formidable soldier.

'Are you on leave for long, sir?'

'I have three months, unless I'm called back. I intend to take the time to find an estate. However, my first task is to replace the horse I lost at the last battle.'

That was something she could help him with. She'd supplied several horses to military gentleman in the past. 'I might have exactly what you're looking for, Colonel Wescott. I can send . . . '

His lips thinned. His annoyance was barely contained and his expression frosty. 'I thank you for your offer, Miss Peterson, but I'm sure I shall manage to acquire what I want without a young lady's assistance.'

She swallowed back her angry retort. What a disagreeable man! He must know she was an expert in the matter of horseflesh, after all had she not demonstrated this yesterday? The splendid matching chestnuts that pulled her

16

carriage were from her own stud and the excellent bays Edward owned had been selected by her.

Her first opinion of this gentleman had been correct. He was objectionable. Ignoring the colonel, she called out to her brother-in-law. 'Edward, if you will excuse me, I must go upstairs. I have promised to spend time with Ellen and my nephews this morning.'

His expression of relief was quite comical. He must have believed he was about to become embroiled in a disagreement between herself and his unpleasant brother. He was arrogant, autocratic and not half as nice as Edward. She was sorely tempted to find an excuse to return immediately to Bracken Hall.

* * *

The evening was much as she had expected. Lydia was so used to speaking her mind on politics or other matters, she found it impossible to remain silent. Frequently she interjected in the gentlemen's discussion and her shin was sore from the kicks she received each time from Ellen.

By the time they rose to leave the gentleman to their port, Lydia was aware she and Simon Westcott were of a similar mind. They held each other in cordial dislike. He, no doubt, thought her opinionated and unfeminine, but she knew him to be overbearing and arrogant.

So matters were equal on that score.

No sooner was the door closed behind them than her sister turned to her in distress. 'Lydia, what were you thinking of? Could you not see how much you were annoying Simon? We did so wish you to get on.'

Lydia embraced her. 'I apologise, my love. I know you and Edward intended us to make a match. It would never do, you know. We disliked each other on sight. I'm afraid you and Edward must forget your machinations. I shall do my best to be civil to him but shall avoid his company when I can. After all, I'm here to spend time with you and the boys, not wait for an offer from Simon Westcott.'

A Dangerous Ride

Lydia managed to remain apart from her new relative by spending her days with her nephews and her sister. She exercised her mare at dawn before anyone had risen, riding to the nearby park where they could both let off pent-up energy. However, she had no option but to dine with him each evening.

Each night she did her best to remain silent when the gentlemen were discussing subjects considered unsuitable for ladies. But every night she found herself sharing her own views, provoked beyond reason, quite often by Edward. If she did not know him to be the kindest man alive she would have thought he was deliberately goading her to be at loggerheads with his brother.

Fortunately the colonel was as assiduous in his avoidance tactics as she. He spent the days viewing suitable geldings and eventually purchased one. He sang its praises at dinner. The animal was, according to him, a prince among horses. Brutus was five years old and obedient to bit and heel, with powerful hindquarters and shoulders ideal for him to take back to France with him. She got up early the next morning in order to examine this paragon for herself.

Undoing the loose box, she attached a lead rope and led the enormous horse into the yard where she tethered him to a metal ring.

'Well, old fellow, let's have a look at you. You're certainly a handsome one and well up to your master's weight.'

The gelding lowered his massive head and breathed noisily in her face. She took this opportunity to push back his lips and examine his mouth. As she was so doing, the man she'd hoped to avoid strolled into the yard.

'Miss Peterson, you've come to admire my animal, I see. I believe my guineas to be well spent.'

'And I know that they were not. This horse is not what you were told.' She braced herself to receive a pithy response.

He drew himself to his full height, his mouth thinned and two spots of colour appeared like warning flags on his cheeks.

'Miss Peterson, I'm obliged to you for offering your opinion on my recent purchase. I pride myself on being an expert in this field, but, of course, I bow to your superior knowledge.'

His sarcasm was uncalled for. She had been about to apologise, to make light of her comment that the huge bay gelding was nearer fifteen years of age than five. However, his attitude goaded her into further comment.

'Colonel Westcott have you ever heard the expression long in the tooth? This gelding has had his teeth filed. If you look closely at his gums you will observe the discrepancy. A horse, of the age you think this one is, would not have so much tooth showing.'

His hands clenched. He no doubt wished to berate her for having the temerity to offer a comment in an area that was strictly a gentleman's preserve. Her palm was resting gently on the neck of the animal and he detected her unease. Immediately his ears flattened. Before she could warn him, the aforementioned teeth buried themselves in Westcott's arm.

The resulting pandemonium allowed her to escape. Her ears were burning from his immoderate language. No doubt the gelding would be returned as unsound but that would be unfair. The bay was a little past his prime but was obviously an intelligent animal and ideal for a soldier.

Without stopping to consider the possible consequences she spun, her blue-velvet riding habit swirling around her booted feet. He needed to be persuaded to keep the bay. Fortunately, the swearing had ceased and the gentleman in question had hold of his horse. To her astonishment, he was rubbing the animal's nose with affection.

Perhaps this man was not such an arrogant, objectionable creature as she had at first surmised if he could forgive his mount for savaging him.

*   *   *

Simon smiled ruefully as he rubbed his injured shoulder.

'Well, Brutus, I got my comeuppance from you!'

The horse lipped his hand in apology.

Good God! The wretched girl was correct. How could he have been so gullible? He'd taken a cursory glance at the bay's mouth and been fooled. He could legitimately return his purchase and demand a refund of his guineas.

No, the gelding might not be the youngster he'd imagined, but he was more than adequate for his needs and he liked the way the animal had protected the girl.

A slight movement in the archway attracted his attention. He glanced up to see her watching him. He hid his smile; he might dislike the chit intensely but he could not fault her courage.

'Jenkins, fetch the tack. I shall take Brutus to the park for a gallop.'

As he waited for his groom, he considered the young woman who'd almost made him lose his temper. She was nothing like Edward's wife. Lady Grayson and Miss Peterson were as different as chalk is to cheese. Ellen was dainty, with blue eyes and golden hair and the sweetest nature one could wish for. Her younger sister was a wildcat. She did have remarkable green eyes and abundant nut brown hair, but that was all there was to recommend her. The girl was overly tall and her features nondescript. One wouldn't exactly call her bracket-faced, but she was no beauty, that was for sure. Small wonder she was still unwed.

His own accumulated wealth and impeccable pedigree meant he was much sought-after by the matchmaking matrons he encountered on the continent. Being a soldier gave him the excuse of duty to his country when he wished to remove himself from possible entrapment.

He swung into the saddle and clattered out of the yard, heading for Hyde Park. So early in the day there would be few people taking the air at this time of the morning.

★ ★ ★

Lydia waited until the colonel had left the yard before hurrying back. She always went out at this time and had no idea he would be there this morning with the same intention. She was tempted to forget to return to her chamber and not risk a second confrontation. However, that would not be fair to Pegasus; her mare was in need of the exercise.

How could anyone prefer the noise, the smell and restriction of the city?

The tranquillity of her estate in Essex, where she was surrounded by horses, could dress in breeches and boots and ride astride, was heaven to her. Making inane small talk to overperfumed strangers in rooms so suffocatingly hot it was surprising more women did not swoon was a pastime she abhorred.

Billy grinned at her over the loose box. 'Take care this morning, miss. Them cobbles will be a mite slippery until the sun's up.'

'Thank you, Billy. I shall come to no harm. Peg's as surefooted as a mountain goat. I'll take it slowly through the streets and not allow her to trot until we're on the grass.'

She guided the mare expertly through the archway that led to the street. Her sister would be horrified if she knew there was no groom accompanying her. But as Ellen never rose before noon, and avoided the stable yard at all times, she was unlikely to hear about her breach of etiquette.

The railings outside the house were

coated in frost and the trees similarly adorned. How beautiful everything looked in the early-morning sunlight. The pavements were empty apart from servants on errands. This area of London was mercifully free from street traders and hawkers, and none of the residents of these grand houses would dream of being seen about so early.

Pegasus knew her way to the park. They took the same route every morning they were in town. They entered without having met another rider. She paused on the grass, gazing in delight at the trees. Everything appeared as if covered in diamonds. What a beautiful morning; too good to be cooped up in London.

Even in the park the air was tainted, the smell of coal smoke never far away. Imagine what the East End must be like, where poor folk teemed in dwellings she would not house an animal in. She stared across the empty landscape. How could there be anything wrong in this enchanted world?

Her horse shifted beneath her, shaking her head impatiently, eager to be off. 'Yes, Peg, I know. You want to stretch your legs. However, sweetheart, we shall take it steady until I know how hard the ground is.'

She touched the mare's flank with her heel, settled into the saddle, and enjoyed the smooth canter. She knew even the lightest touch would push her mount into a headlong gallop.

There was no sign of the colonel ahead. He must have ridden in the other direction. She cantered up the avenue of trees into the open land. She could not resist the temptation; the going was good, ideal for her purpose. She shortened the reins and gave her mare a signal.

Tears whipped from her eyes. The speed was exhilarating and the way in front clear for another mile. Pegasus lived up to her name, flying across the ground, head outstretched, ears forward, enjoying the race as much as she.

Lydia was aware the lake was just

ahead. Time to slow down, her five minutes of freedom were over. She settled in the saddle, pulling gently on the reins to remind Peg to reduce her speed, when, from nowhere, a horse thundered alongside and an arm reached out and snatched her from the saddle.

Good grief! She was being abducted. Ellen had warned her many times not to ride alone, that there were dangerous men lurking in the isolated areas of the park. She had only one chance to save herself, if she struggled she might fall to her death. But if she could dislodge the man who was holding her across his pommel it would be he who suffered not her.

Thanking God for the hours she'd spent perfecting her riding skills, she buried her hands in the wiry black mane of her abductor's horse. With the agility of a circus performer she pressed down, whilst swinging her weight sideways. Her hips thumped into the villain, unbalancing him. She pushed backwards and the arm around her waist was gone. She was free.

Her heart was thundering as loudly as the hooves on the hard ground. Could she twist herself into the saddle without falling? This manoeuvre would have been impossible were she not wearing a habit with a divided skirt. Flinging herself backwards, releasing her grip on the mane, she managed to bring her left leg across the horse's withers. Gripping hard with her knees, she regained her balance and was upright in the saddle.

'Steady boy, steady.' The horse responded to her soothing voice and the mad gallop became a smooth extended canter. She was riding without reins or stirrups, but was confident the animal was responding to her voice and the pressure of her legs.

'Good lad, good boy, the race is over. It's time to walk. She patted the animal's lathered neck and grabbed the flapping reins. She pulled firmly and her mount responded. A sudden rhythmic

31

pounding alongside made the horse shy. This time she was not so fortunate and flew from the saddle.

Her world upended and the breath was knocked from her lungs. She lay still, waiting for her head to stop spinning. Had she broken any limbs? Would her abductor recover first and reach her before she could escape?

She must make an effort.

She opened her eyes to discover she was lying between eight equine legs, four grey and four brown. Using her own mount to brace herself she slowly regained her feet. She collapsed against the neck of the bay, shock making her incapable of thought. Her composure returned and she began to take stock. Surely this horse was known to her? It was Brutus, Colonel Westcott's new mount. Sick with dread, she stumbled forward to peer between the two animals. Her worst fears were realised. The colonel was spread-eagled on the ground several hundred yards away.

Lydia could scarcely grasp the

enormity of the tragedy. Brutus, he was a brave soldier, he did not deserve to end so ignominiously. How am I going to tell Edward that I have murdered his brother?

He might be alive, hadn't she survived the fall, why should he not have done the same? After all, was he not a battle scarred veteran? She must ride back, not stand here procrastinating. There was little point in remounting, she would lead both horses. However her legs refused to obey her command. She was trembling like a blancmange, doubtful she could travel even that short distance without collapsing.

By lengthening the stirrup leather she managed to scramble into her mare's saddle. She leant across and pulled the reins over the gelding's head.

'Come along, Brutus, we must see if we can help your master.'

Then, to her astonishment, what she had taken to be a corpse rolled over and stood up. Relief flooded through her he was unharmed. Then her relief turned to fear. If he had been angry earlier that day, what might be his reaction now?

She would not wait to discover. She would leave whilst his back was turned, flee to the safety of her apartment and remain there until he had calmed down. Dropping the gelding's reins in front of him, she raced away, expecting to hear a roar of rage behind her.

In her desire to put as much distance between herself and the colonel, she had not stopped to consider that maybe Brutus was not trained to stand when his reins were dropped. When she halted at the park gates she realised his horse had accompanied her.

If he had been enraged before, now he would be incandescent.

*　*　*

Lydia hesitated for a second. Despite Simon's bewildering actions and the fact that it was his own fault he was injured, she could hardly expect him to walk home. She leant across to gather up the trailing reins.

'You're a silly boy, Brutus. Have you no shame? It's your duty to stay with your master at all times. Come along, we must go back and help the colonel.'

She ached in every bone and twice almost slipped from the saddle. She pulled the gelding closer, kicked her boot from the single stirrup of her side saddle and prepared to transfer to the other horse. This was a trick she'd accomplished many times before, but always in the safety of her own paddock and not when she was recovering from a thumping fall.

With one hand braced on the withers of her mare she swung her right leg out, dropping safely astride the colonel's horse.

There was no need to lead her mare; the animal would follow her anywhere. Brutus was a massive beast but this did not bother her. She urged him into a canter toward the open ground where she'd last seen the gentleman. She expected to meet him striding in her direction.

Where was the wretched man? The park was deserted, the landscape empty.

He had vanished into thin air. She scanned the ground. Had she mistaken the spot? Her hands clenched. Here was evidence indeed. The grass was flattened, the frost melted from his body heat, but what was worse, there were splashes of red amongst the white.

★　★　★

Simon was a soldier, he'd suffered worse injuries in the past and continued to wield his sword. He couldn't run, but he could jog. If he walked twenty paces and then jogged he would arrive soon enough. His head was fuzzy, the pain behind his eyes making it hard to concentrate. He would never forgive himself if any harm had come to that young woman.

Despite his discomfort, his lips twitched. He loved the way her eyes flashed when she was enraged. Somehow he arrived at the slope that led down to the lake. His stomach twisted. There was no sign of either horse or rider. He was too late. He stumbled a few steps down the slope to collapse in despair.

Moments later he recovered his wits. The ice on the surface of the water was unbroken. No drowning had taken place here. His spirits soared, the girl was safe. He hadn't caused her death by his foolhardy attempt to rescue her. Flopping back on the ground he let the dizziness take him. His eyes closed and he slipped into oblivion.

★　★　★

Lydia stood up in the stirrups, surveying the horizon. There was only one place he could be . . . the lake. She kicked Brutus on, her heart racing. Had he staggered in a daze to the edge and tumbled down the slope to meet his death in the freezing water?

Reining in, she flung herself to the ground, the impact sending waves of pain shooting up her legs. She clung to the saddle to steady herself.

She peered down the slope and saw him lying, eyes closed, a blood-soaked cloth roughly tied around his forehead. He was unconscious.

She half ran, half fell, to his side. Dropping to her knees, she placed her fingers under his chin, feeling for a pulse. It was weak, but regular. She had no petticoats to tear to stop the flow of blood from his wound and was at a loss to know how to proceed. He was too heavy to lift so she must rouse him. She slithered to the edge of the water and rubbed the hem of her habit across the ice.

'Colonel Wescott? Can you hear me? You cannot remain here, it's far too cold.'

Gently she rubbed the dampened cloth across his face, praying it would work.

'Sir, I beg you, wake up so that I can assist you to your horse.'

His eyelids flickered and he was

staring back at her.

'Thank heavens! Colonel Wescott, you have fallen from your horse and injured your head. I intend to get you home, but I need your cooperation.'

'Give me a moment, my head's spinning.'

'No, Colonel Wescott, you must not go back to sleep. Get up at once. I thought you a brave soldier. Do not lie here like a coward.' She grasped his arms and pulled him into a sitting position.

'Colonel, you need the attention of a physician urgently. Put your arm around my shoulders and together we shall have you back home in no time.'

He was more or less unconscious, but assisted as best he could. The ride back was a nightmare. She was obliged to hold him steady in order to prevent him from crashing to the cobbles.

'Jenkins, Billy, come at once. Colonel Wescott has taken a tumble and he's in a bad way.'

The clatter of boots heralded the

arrival of both men, and without further ado they lifted the injured man from his saddle. It took a further two grooms to assist them in transporting him to the house.

Edward was down and took charge. 'You're a brave girl. My brother might well owe his life to you. Now, my dear, leave matters to me. You must take care of yourself. I shall send word to you after the doctor has visited.'

Martha was instantly at her side.

'My word, Miss Peterson, whatever next? Your lovely habit is quite ruined and there's blood all over it. Are you injured? Did you take a tumble?'

Lydia was too tired to explain. 'Yes, we both fell. Colonel Wescott is badly hurt but I am merely bruised. Is my bath ready? I think a long soak will soon restore me.'

An hour later she was safely in bed, hot bricks at her feet and a breakfast tray across her knees. She'd waited in vain for a message from her brother-in-law. Was his condition so dire Edward had not wished to alarm her? Then someone hurried along the passageway outside and tapped briskly on the door.

'Martha, go at once and see who it is. I'm desperate for news.'

Her brother-in-law hovered in the doorway of her bedchamber, his expression anxious. Her throat constricted. The news must be bad indeed.

'Tell me, Edward, how is the patient?'

'My dear girl, I am concerned about you. I had no idea you had fallen also. I have the physician waiting downstairs. Shall I send him to you?'

'I suffered no lasting harm, sir. I am stiff and sore but will be up and about in an hour or two. Your brother, is he better?'

'Simon's in no danger. He has a nasty gash, which has been sutured, and a slight concussion. He's being instructed to remain in bed for a few days, but knowing him he will be up tomorrow showing no ill effects from his experience.'

'Thank heavens! Did he tell you what happened?'

He shook his head. 'He did not, my dear. Simon says he has no recollection of the accident. I was hoping you could enlighten me. How did you come to fall as well? I can't imagine how such expert riders came to grief in this way.'

How could she tell him what had happened when she scarcely understood it herself? Far better to prevaricate and wait until she'd spoken to the colonel.

'I'm sorry, it's too distressing to talk about. I have a frightful headache. Please forgive me. I do not feel able to continue the conversation at present.'

'Of course, my dear girl. I shall leave you to rest. Nothing matters apart from the fact that you are both relatively unharmed. Time enough to discuss the details when you're fully restored.'

She closed her eyes, her cheeks pink, waiting until he'd left the chamber to sit up. She hated to deceive him, but could not reveal Wescott's part in the accident. She was at a loss to know what had prompted his extraordinary behaviour. She would like go to his apartment as soon as he was well enough for visitors and ask him why he'd snatched her from the saddle.

'Martha, please close the shutters and draw the bed hangings. If Lady Grayson asks for me, could you tell her that I'm sleeping?'

Her maid tutted under her breath, unimpressed by her deceit.

★ ★ ★

Simon waited impatiently for his brother to return with news of the girl. He was indebted to her. He could think of no other female of his acquaintance who could have accomplished what she had this morning.

However, it did not alter the fact that her behaviour had caused him to fall. He'd said nothing to Edward — he must get matters straight before he revealed what had actually happened.

Despite his headache, his mouth curved. He understood why his sister-in-law had been so insistent that Lydia

43

visited whilst he was there. For some unfathomable reason, she believed the two of them could make a match. Ellen was correct; they were similar in some ways, both strong willed, preferring the outdoor life to prancing around in overheated ballrooms dressed in fine silks and satins. Lydia was as brave as a soldier, had a sharp wit and grasp of matters he'd often seen his officers fail to understand. If he was honest, he was beginning to like her very much.

The door to his bedchamber opened and Edward strolled in.

'You look a good deal better, Simon. Your pallor has receded. How is the head?' He perched on the edge of the bed. 'I'm delighted to tell you, old fellow, that the heroine of the hour insists she is only bruised. She was unable to explain how both of you came to be unseated. Perhaps you can enlighten me?'

'I had not intended to discuss it until I had clarified matters with her. However, I shall tell you the whole and see if you can explain the unexplainable.'

His brother listened. By the end of the tale he was, much to Simon's consternation, laughing heartily.

'Good grief! What a numbskull you are, Simon. Do you not listen to anything I tell you? Lydia is an expert horsewoman. I told you she runs a stud with her younger brother. She must have believed you were a stranger trying to abduct her. Why would she have thought you were attempting to save her from a bolting horse?'

'I cannot credit that a young woman, even someone as fearless as she, could remain sufficiently calm to deliberately tip me out of the saddle.'

'That's exactly what must have happened. There's no other logical explanation. I have no sympathy for you. If you'd broken your neck that would have served you right. However, this does not explain how Lydia came to fall.'

'When I fell, she was face down across the pommel. She must have slipped to the ground. I owe her an apology, as well as my gratitude.' He chuckled. 'She already considers me an overbearing man. I wonder how she'll greet my serving of humble pie?'

'You shall have to wait until tomorrow to find out. I'll leave you to rest. I cannot wait to tell Ellen what you did.'

His brother left him but it was difficult to sleep. Until he had made things right between himself and his rescuer and was certain she was unharmed from her fall, he would be unable to settle. He could not recall having been so agitated about a young lady before.

* * *

By lunchtime, Lydia was more than ready to stir. She could not speak to the colonel. Even she drew the line at visiting a gentleman in his bedchamber. She had promised her nephews a trip to Hatchard's bookshop; this afternoon would be the ideal time to do so.

Her maid was in the dressing-room. 'Martha, I wish to get up. I have some

46

errands for the chambermaid to run.'

Dressed in a becoming buttercup-yellow gown, the waist fashionably high and the skirt full enough to walk with ease, she surveyed her reflection in the full-length glass.

'I don't look too bad considering what happened earlier. I shall wear the matching pelisse and kid half boots.'

'What about your new bonnet? You have not worn that at all since Lady Grayson purchased it for you last week.'

'I shall never wear that monstrosity. Good heavens, Martha, it looks more like a coal scuttle than something to wear on one's head. No, I shall wear my usual bonnet; the ribbons match my ensemble.' She picked up her reticule and pulled on her long calfskin gloves. 'What can be keeping the boys? I heard the carriage drawing up in front a moment ago. If they do not join me within the next five minutes we shall leave without them.'

With Martha hurrying behind her, she headed for the vestibule. Two small boys, miniatures of their father, raced to meet her at the bottom of the stairs, ignoring the remonstrations of their nursemaid.

'Aunt Lydia, you've been an age. We've been waiting here for hours and hours.'

'Arthur, I believe you are exaggerating. I understood you to be coming to my apartment. I have been standing there for a week at least. That is why I am late.'

George, a replica of his brother, threw his arms around her knees.

'I love you, Aunt Lydia. You are the bestest fun of anyone I know.'

'And I love you both, you are my favourite nephews.'

'You don't have any other ones.'

'That's enough, Master Arthur. Miss Peterson is waiting to leave, so stop your tomfoolery right now.'

The visit to the bookshop was a resounding success. The boys had, amongst other books, a copy of *Robinson Crusoe* and she a new novel called *Pride and Prejudice*. She'd also bought some writing requisites for herself and drawing paper and paints for the boys. These parcels were neatly packaged, secured with string and sitting beneath the squabs.

The carriage lurched and the coachman yelled for his horses to halt. Immediately Arthur was on his feet and lowering the window to hang out like an urchin.

'Sit down at once, Master Arthur, it's not seemly to hang out like that.'

The little boy ignored her. 'Look, George, there's a man running away.'

The nursemaid reached out to remove her charge. 'Come along, young sir, do as you're bid'

Her words were lost as Arthur screamed in agony.

A Truce

The little boy crashed backwards, clutching his nose from which copious quantities of blood was pouring.

'Keep still, Arthur, we must stem the flow of blood.' There was no need for Lydia to rip up her petticoat to use as a cloth, for both Martha and the nursemaid produced linen squares from their reticules.

'Let me deal with this, Miss Peterson, or you will spoil a second gown.' Martha was already on her knees, supporting the child with one hand and holding a folded linen square to his nose with the other.

'Aunt Lydia, won't Arthur have empty legs if he bleeds so much?' George asked.

'No, my love, a nose bleed seems far worse than it is. See, it's stopping now.'

The groom appeared at the window.

'Is everything all right in here, Miss Peterson?'

'Yes, Master Arthur has a nose bleed. Tell Tom to return as swiftly as possible to Brook Street.'

The groom vanished and the carriage rocked as the horses were urged into a brisk trot. Tom drove around the stationary vehicles in front. As he cracked his whip, the groom shouted for unwary pedestrians to remove themselves from their path.

The swaying and bouncing jarred every bone in her bruised body. Arthur was back on the seat, revelling in his dramatic accident.

'Something hit me in the face! Did you see, Aunt Lydia?'

His brother shoved him. 'Serves you right. If you hadn't opened the window, it wouldn't have happened.'

'That's enough boys. Hold on tight or there shall be a second accident.'

★ ★ ★

Simon was determined to get up. 'Sam, fetch my robe. I'm not mouldering in my bed a moment longer. I shall sit in a chair by the window and watch the world go by in the street below.'

His man hurried from the dressing-room. 'It ain't wise, Colonel, the quack told you to stay put. That's a nasty knock on the head you've got, and you ain't no lightweight. You collapse on the floor, then you'll have to stop there, that's for sure.'

His man had been with him these past ten years and was more of a friend than a valet. He'd accompanied him across the peninsula, making sure his billet was reasonable, his food what there was of it well cooked and ready when he returned, exhausted, from battle. This gave him the right to speak to him informally.

'Fair enough, I'll take my chances. Let me lean on your shoulder; my legs are none too steady.' With considerable relief, he collapsed into a winged armchair. Sam was right. He would have been better off staying where he was. He'd not been sitting there long when he saw the Grayson carriage rattling towards the house. The occupants must feel as if they were being tossed about in a storm.

The carriage rocked to a standstill at the front of the house. Their precipitous arrival had been observed by Ellen, who had been waiting by the drawing-room window for their return. Lydia waved gaily, hoping to indicate there was nothing seriously wrong.

'Your mama is watching, boys. Pray do not make too much of the accident. We have no wish to alarm her. Remember, she is in a delicate condition and must not be upset.' The new baby was expected next month.

'We promise, Aunt Lydia,' the little boys replied.

Her sister greeted them with dismay. 'Good heavens, Lydia, disaster, as always, appears to be following you about. Did Arthur fall from the seat?'

'I didn't, Mama, I promise. Something

came in the window and hit me on the nose. See, I'm covered in blood.'

'Indeed I can see, young man. You shall have a fine black eye as well. Now, run along upstairs with your nursemaid and let Nanny clean you up. Come down to the small drawing-room when you are presentable. I shall have Cook prepare a delicious tea for us all.'

The children scampered off, leaving the poor nursemaid to keep up as best she could. Lydia smiled.

'Ellen, I cannot credit that twice in one day I have been covered in someone else's blood. Arthur was quite correct. We had halted because of some altercation just ahead, and a passerby threw in a stone which hit Arthur fair and square.'

'Never mind, my love. The incident was not your fault. Neither accident reflects on you in any way. The colonel is much recovered, by the by, and is determined to get up tomorrow. For some reason, he's most insistent you should join him in the library tomorrow morning at nine o'clock.' She smiled archly, and tapped Lydia on the arm. 'I believe you've made a conquest, I can think of no other reason he should wish to speak to you alone unless he intends to make you an offer.'

Lydia recoiled, catching her heel in the hem of her gown as she did so.

'Botheration! See what you made me do, Ellen. Not only have I ruined my pelisse, I've torn my gown as well.' Recovering her composure she stared crossly at her sister. 'You're talking nonsense. Colonel Westcott dislikes me as much as I dislike him. He wishes to thank me for my part in his rescue, nothing more.'

She stomped back to her apartment, her sister's annoying laughter following her. Surely she'd not been mistaken in her assessment? They had done nothing but argue since they'd met last week. She believed that society was unfair to women and allowed them no freedom to live their lives. He believed a gentleman's prerogative was to take control and that a female was incapable of making a rational decision or running her own life successfully.

She snorted inelegantly, startling two footmen who were balanced precariously on stools, dusting the picture rails. She fixed them with a stony glare and they hastily resumed their work. How she hated being constantly observed! She longed to return home where she was free to roam about her estate without being gawped at by overzealous servants.

* * *

Simon roared for his man and Sam came bustling in.

'You want to go back to bed, sir?'

'No, I don't, Sam Smith. I want you to go downstairs at once and see why my nephews and Miss Peterson have returned in such disarray. Some mishap has befallen them. I wish to know what it was.'

He closed his eyes, waiting for the

pounding in his head to subside. An image of the girl danced behind his lids. When his manservant returned and told him the tale, he laughed.

'I think I shall return to my bed. Whatever I say, do not let me get up until tomorrow. I wish to be dressed and downstairs by nine o'clock. I have an appointment with Miss Peterson that I do not intend to miss.'

★ ★ ★

Martha was awaiting her return. 'If you give me your garments, Miss Peterson, I shall soak them in milk immediately. With luck the stains will come out.'

'I'm sorry to say, Martha, but I've also torn the hem. Perhaps it would be better if I remained in bed the rest of the day. I cannot imagine what other disasters might befall me before the sun sets.'

She had eaten nothing since she rose and the thought of Cook's freshly baked scones and strawberry conserve drew her to the small drawing-room. She was crossing the vast hall when the butler accosted her.

'Excuse me, Miss Peterson, where would you like your purchases to go?'

The books. She'd quite forgotten about them in the excitement of the accident.

'The drawing paper, paints and children's books go to the schoolroom, please, Foster. The rest can go on the bookcase in my sitting-room.'

Forgetting about the books, she headed for the chattering and laughter she could hear along the corridor.

★ ★ ★

The following morning, Lydia dressed in her freshly sponged habit. She couldn't ride before meeting the colonel in the library but would go immediately afterwards.

As she crossed the vast entrance hall, she heard raised voices coming from the library. Surely that was her brother-in-law? Something was amiss. The double doors were standing open and the butler, Foster, was dithering in the doorway wringing his hands. She stepped around the agitated man and walked in.

Her eyes widened. A scene of devastation greeted her. Books were strewn all over the floor, tables and chairs upturned and the French doors at the far end of the room swung wildly from broken hinges.

'Good gracious! We have been burgled.' Identical heads turned and both men stared at her. Westcott answered, his eyes glinting with amusement. He looked remarkably robust for a man with eight stitches in his wound.

'Miss Peterson, how observant you are. We should not have noticed had you not pointed this out to us.'

She giggled. 'The blow to your head has obviously addled your wits, sir. The question was rhetorical. But why? What on earth were they looking for?'

Lord Grayson frowned. 'That's what

we were discussing, my dear. The internal doors were not locked. They could have progressed further and stolen something of value. For some reason, they remained in here.'

'Perhaps they feared they were about to be discovered, Edward.'

'That seems the likely explanation. In future I shall insist Foster closes the shutters every night. The rooms that face the garden are usually left unbarred, only the front of the house is secured in this way.'

She shivered. The icy blast coming in through the broken doors made the room decidedly unpleasant.

'I shall help restore the room later. I know where most of the volumes go.' She bent down and retrieved a book on the flora and fauna of Suffolk. 'I think the damage is minimal. It looks far worse than it is.'

The colonel raised an eyebrow and she waited for his riposte. None was forthcoming this time. Instead he smiled. For some reason, her insides somersaulted and her toes curled in her boots.

'Thank you for your offer, my dear, but I doubt you will be able to. I quite forgot, your head stable lad is downstairs in the kitchen. He arrived an hour ago. I believe there is some emergency at home. Your brother wishes you to return as soon as possible.'

'Thank you, Edward. I shall speak to him at once.'

Not waiting to hear more, she ran from the room, taking the back stairs to the basement kitchen. Her favourite mare was due to foal next month. She must be the emergency.

She burst into the kitchen and Fred scrambled to his feet and touched his forelock.

'Fred, tell me at once why I am required home today?'

'Black Bess is showing signs of premature foaling, Miss Peterson. The master thinks it would be best if you returned. The mare will not settle without you at her side.'

'I can be ready in an hour or two. I must speak to Lady Grayson and say goodbye to my nephews before I leave. That should allow your mount time to recover. Have you spoken to Billy?'

The young man nodded vigorously. 'I have, miss. Will you be travelling in Lord Grayson's carriage?'

'I sincerely hope so. I took a tumble yesterday and am not up to riding thirty miles.' There was another thing she must do as well. She had to speak to the colonel.

The two men were waiting for her in the passageway.

'Can I have the carriage, my lord? The emergency is as I thought, a mare in difficulty.'

'You can, my dear. We shall not be requiring the vehicle today. You will not leave without speaking to Ellen, I hope?'

'Of course not. I shall go and change and get Martha to pack. We must leave as soon as we can. The lanes in our part of Essex make slow going for a coach.'

A slight cough attracted her attention. 'I shall wait for you in the small drawing-room, Miss Peterson. I trust you will spare me a few minutes of your time before you leave?'

She flushed. 'Yes, Colonel Westcott, I'll be with you directly. I intend to breakfast before I depart.'

She was with him in less than a quarter of an hour, which obviously surprised him for he was lounging on the day bed with his boots on the seat. He jumped to his feet and bowed formally. She dropped a neat curtsy and waved him back to his position.

'Miss Peterson, there are two things I must say to you. First, I owe you my most sincere apologies. My brother told me you were an expert horsewoman but I did not believe him. I thought your grey was bolting with you and snatched you from the saddle in order to save you.'

'That is as I thought, sir, a misunderstanding. I took you to be an abductor. I should never have unseated you otherwise.'

'Good, we are making progress. But far more important, I owe you my life. If you had not got me back on my feet and home, I might well have perished before anyone could return to assist me.' He was leaning forward, his dark blue eyes holding her captive.

'Helping you was the least I could do. You would not have been in that predicament but for my actions.'

'In that case, let us cry quits. Perhaps we could start again? We have been at daggers drawn this past week. I would much prefer to be on good terms with you.

This seemed harmless enough. After all, was she not about to depart for the country? 'That will be quite acceptable. I can assure you my nature is not to be argumentative.'

His eyebrows vanished beneath his hair and he made a strange choking sound. Was he laughing at her? Her eyes narrowed, preparing to do battle. Then she relaxed; he was quite right to be amused. She was the most volatile of females, her temper mercurial, and she had been about to fly into the boughs yet again.

'I do not blame you for laughing, Colonel, but I promise I shall endeavour to do better in future. I will learn to curb my tongue . . . '

'Pray, do not do that, my dear girl. Your unpredictability is what I find so . . . so interesting.'

Lydia scrambled to her feet. She found his charm unsettling. He was much easier to deal with when he was on his high horse.

'If you will excuse me, I must eat before I leave.'

'I shall join you.'

They strolled in perfect harmony to the breakfast parlour. She watched in amazement as he piled his plate with ham, coddled eggs, tomatoes and mushrooms. Small wonder he was such a large gentleman; he had a prodigious appetite.

★ ★ ★

Simon was sorry to see Miss Peterson depart. How could he have ever thought of her as unattractive? He wished to further his acquaintance and had every intention of following her to the country when he had completed his visit in town.

He smiled wryly. He rather thought he'd been hoisted by his own petard. He had pushed Miss Peterson away by his foul behaviour when she was perhaps the girl he'd been looking for all his life and never thought to meet. He felt decidedly flat and his head was still painful. Perhaps he would do as Edward suggested and retire to his apartment for the remainder of the day. He was on his way up the grand staircase when there was an insistent knocking at the front door.

He paused, curious as to who should be in such a hurry to be admitted. Foster opened the door and two men stepped in.

He recognized them both. What on earth were Devereux and Dawkins doing here? The last time he'd bumped into them they'd been involved in clandestine activities, searching for a spy who was feeding information to the French.

High Drama

The carriage was making good progress when Billy appeared alongside and tapped on the window. Lydia lowered it.

'Excuse me, miss, but there's a bad storm approaching. Black clouds so low I reckon you can touch them. We ought to find shelter before it hits us.'

'Good gracious! There could be a blizzard; the wind is icy enough. Is there anywhere we can turn off this narrow lane?'

The coachman called down from the box. 'There's a field ahead, Miss Peterson. I can see a barn we could use. The gate into the field is more than wide enough. We can shelter the animals and ourselves, but the carriage will have to take its chance outside.'

She sank back on to the squabs. 'What a nuisance, Martha. Mr Peterson will be expecting me. I hope we are not obliged to waste too much time. It would seem that this journey is plagued by difficulties, I sincerely hope Lord Grayson's splendid new carriage is not damaged as mine was.'

She was concerned that Black Bess might have injured herself in her absence. The mare was naturally fractious and especially so when in foal. Martha pulled the window up and hooked the leather strap on the peg.

'I've never seen the like of them clouds, miss. The sooner we're out of it the better.'

The carriage lurched when a particularly strong gust caught the side as they were turning. Martha, who had been unbalanced, tumbled backwards into the well of the carriage. Laughing, Lydia helped her maid back to the seat. They arrived at the barn not a moment too soon. By the time the horses had been unharnessed and led into the ramshackle building the storm was upon them. Hailstones the size of pebbles rattled down, sending Fred, the groom who had come to fetch Lydia, scurrying for cover. He pulled the door of the barn shut shaking his riding cape to rid himself of the icy pellets.

'It sounds as though someone is hurling missiles at the roof, I hope the carriage will come to no harm.'

Tom grinned and touched his fore-lock. 'I reckon your Jim is well out of this. I wouldn't mind a few weeks with me feet up meself.'

The horses were munching content-edly on a pile of a hay that had been left over from the last harvest. At the far end of the barn, there was a gap in the tiles through which the hail was pouring.

Lydia walked over and kicked it. 'This is unusual. It must be a freak occurrence.' She leant down and picked up a handful. 'Look at this, Billy, some of them are the size of the clay marbles I used to own when I was small.'

'I reckon anyone out in this could be seriously harmed worse than being hit by musket fire.'

Lydia laughed. 'Not quite as bad, but it certainly sounds like we're being attacked.'

They were obliged to remain inside for a further hour. Eventually the storm passed and Tom went out to check that the carriage was undamaged so they could continue their journey. Billy accompanied him. The young man returned, shaking his head.

'Bad news, miss. Them hail stones took the glass clean out of the carriage windows. The wretched stuff is everywhere. Embedded in the seats, the floor. It ain't safe for you to travel inside, that's for certain.'

Lydia had to see for herself. Perhaps the young man was exaggerating. Unfortunately, his prognosis was correct. The inside of the carriage was quite ruined. The sun appeared, the strange hailstorm gone as if it had never happened. Without the thick coating of white upon the grass she would have believed it to have been a figment of her imagination.

'I have to get back. There must be some way we can accomplish this.' She closed her eyes for a moment. 'I have it. Billy, you take Fred up behind you on Pegasus, his mount has already been hard pressed today, he could not take a double burden. I shall ride him and Martha can squeeze up on the box between Tom and the groom.

'I doubt your sidesaddle will fit him, Miss Peterson.'

'I realise that, thank you, Fred. I shall ride astride. Now, please get my trunk down from the rear of the carriage and bring it into the barn. I will only take a few minutes to change then we can be on our way.'

The men busied themselves with the horses whilst Martha unbuckled the trunk and Lydia helped her maid remove the dividing tray that rested on top of the clothes. This was full of the books Lydia had purchased at Hatchard's.

She stripped off her travelling gown and cloak and stepped into her divided habit. As always she was wearing her riding boots. Whilst her maid was folding up the garments and replacing them in the trunk, Lydia glanced down idly at the books stacked on the dirt. There was a small black volume amongst them that she didn't recognise.

Curiously, she picked it up. Where had this book of sermons come from? There was no time to investigate further as Billy shouted that they were ready to leave. Quickly pushing the small volume into her skirt pocket, she hurried out. The weather was far too cold to leave the horses standing.

'I'm ready. As soon as the trunk is strapped on we can be on our way.'

They were only an hour from home when there was a further setback. The gelding she was riding went lame.

'Botheration! Billy, can you dismount and check his foot? I believe there is a stone lodged inside the shoe. Fred, tell the coach to continue. We'll catch up once this matter has been sorted.'

The wind had got up again and she

shivered. Fortunately the narrow lane had high hedges on either side which took the brunt of the weather. The two horses were alone on the track and the carriage had vanished around the sharp bend but they could still hear the rattle of the wheels. This was not a good place to be stranded. There had been reports of footpads, disaffected farm workers and ex-soldiers in the vicinity. These men, on finding no employment, had taken to highway robbery.

'Billy, Fred, do you have your pistols primed? The woodland just ahead is where Squire Bentley was waylaid not long ago.'

'We'll do it now, miss. Better safe than sorry.' Billy straightened, brushing the mud from his hands. 'There, done it. He's taken no harm, I've removed the stone.' As he was swinging back into the saddle behind Fred, the air was rent by a hideous sound of gunfire. Martha screamed and the men shouted they were too far away to distinguish what was said.

Her worst fears had come to pass. Her carriage was being held up by brigands.

'Take cover, Miss Peterson. Get behind the hedge where you'll not be seen.' Both men drew their weapons before Fred kicked Pegasus into a gallop.

Lydia dropped to the ground. They'd just passed a gate; she could get into the field through that. This gate was old and hanging from its hinges. The grass was growing over the bottom, making it impossible to open. There was no way to access the meadow unless she jumped it. Was her mount up to the challenge?

Under normal conditions, when he was fresh, he'd have no difficulty clearing such an obstacle. In order to jump this gate he'd have to do it from a virtual standstill.

Pounding feet were approaching. She had no choice. Using the bars to scramble back into the saddle, she gathered the reins and sent a fervent prayer. She patted her mount's sweating neck. 'It's up to you now, Sydney. You've jumped higher than this. I pray you can do so again. I fear my life might depend upon it.'

★ ★ ★

Simon called across the entrance hall. 'Devereux, Dawkins, what on earth are you doing here?'

'Wescott, I'm glad you're still here. My friend, we need your expertise. Is Lord Grayson about? I must speak to him urgently.'

His brother appeared from his study. 'Good morning, gentlemen. I gather you are friends of my brother's. Come to my study. We can be private there.'

Nothing more was said until the study door closed. The matter must be confidential; these two dealt in nothing else but secrets.

'I'll be as brief as I can. Time is of the essence here. You know that Bonaparte is safe on Elba, but supporters are plotting to release him. We have been watching one of them carefully. We knew he was to collect evidence of those involved in the treachery and details of how this scheme was to be accomplished. Somehow the man became aware he was under surveillance and fled. We apprehended him but he no longer had the evidence on him.'

Simon looked at his brother and raised his eyebrows.

'How does this concern us, Dawkins?'

'I was getting to that. By questioning those in the vicinity, we were able to discover your carriage, Lord Grayson, had been seen not far from where we captured the traitor. We found no evidence of the book on the man's person or in the street so we're sincerely hoping it was somehow secreted in your carriage.'

Edward frowned. 'My carriage was thoroughly cleaned. One of my boys was hit in the face by a stone and suffered a nasty nosebleed. There was nothing found inside.'

'I'm not so sure, Edward. The stone Miss Peterson believed had injured Arthur was not discovered. It's possible the missile was the missing book.'

Devereux nodded. 'That sounds logical. Thank heavens! I was beginning to fear we were too late to recover it.'

'I know exactly where it must be. It will be amongst the purchases Miss Peterson made. Unfortunately she's returning to Bracken Hall at this very moment.'

Edward slammed his hand on the desk, making them all jump. 'I say! So that is why my library was ransacked last night. The perpetrators were searching for this volume.'

Simon's stomach somersaulted. 'They'll be after Miss Peterson. There's no time to lose. I'll take Jenkins and Smith and get after them. No, there's no point in arguing, Edward, it's my job. I'm the only one who can reach Miss Peterson in time.'

Leaving Dawkins and Devereux to his brother, he turned and thundered up the stairs three at a time. He burst into his bedchamber, shouting for his man.

'Smith, get a message down to the stables and have Jenkins saddle our mounts. Miss Peterson is in great danger. We must ride at once to her rescue. Pack only my essentials.' He deliberately did not mention the matter of the missing book that was a state secret, not for his servants to know.

In less than one quarter of an hour he was astride Brutus, his sword strapped securely to his side and two pistols rammed into the pockets of his riding coat. His men had rifles secured to their saddles. They had both been chosen men before he'd commandeered them to his personal service. It would be quicker to cut across country. If they ignored the toll roads they could travel faster than the coach and easily overtake them.

God willing, they would not be too late.

* * *

Lydia kicked the gelding hard, throwing her hands and weight forward. The beast responded magnificently. She wrenched the inside rein and dug in with her heels. They soared into the air, clearing the gate by a foot or more to land safely in the meadow. She reined back, tumbling from the saddle, to guide the animal against the hedge.

She prayed that this was dense enough to render her invisible. She could see nothing through the branches; they were too thick to penetrate. But she could hear the footpads. They ran past. Her pulse settled. There had been no further shouting or gunshots from further down the lane.

Her breath caught in her throat. They were returning. If the horse made a sound she would be discovered. She stroked his face and he lowered his head to rest on her shoulder, seemingly able to understand the necessity for quiet.

The two men stopped a few yards from the gate.

'Where's that girl gone? It ain't natural, she's vanished into thin air. I reckon she's turned tail and is galloping back to fetch help.'

'I reckon as you're right, Cal. No point looking when she ain't here. Let's get back to the others. We don't want to be caught. It's a hanging matter, what we've been involved with these past weeks.'

His companion swore. 'Ain't everything a hanging matter? Might as well dangle from a rope earning good money than perish from lifting flimsies from a gent's wallet.'

They were moving away.

There was little of value in the carriage. Maybe they would take the horses and be satisfied with that. Suddenly Sydney pricked up his ears. Before she could prevent it he raised his head and whinnied loudly. Immediately the men were back and scrambling over the gate.

She had no time to remount. It was too late to run.

★　★　★

Simon turned to shout at the two men galloping at his heels. 'I heard shots not far ahead. We're too late to prevent the ambush but we have surprise on our side. We'll gallop straight at them.'

He withdrew his sword. He had to reach the carriage before anyone was hurt. But it was even more imperative to prevent the traitors from retrieving the codebook.

He thundered down the lane and around a sharp bend to find a scene of chaos. A group of men and one woman, were being held at gunpoint by two rough individuals. There was no sign of Miss Peterson. Two other villains had removed the trunk from the back of the carriage and were throwing the contents haphazardly across the path. Hopefully they had not discovered what they sought.

His sudden appearance was enough to tip the matter in his favour. Jenkins and Smith had their rifles pointed at the attackers and he had his sword and pistol ready.

'You men are done here. Stand still. If you wish to live you'll drop your weapons and surrender.'

Four heads swiveled in astonishment. This was enough for two of the captured men to surge forward and disarm them. Jenkins and Sam would take care of things now. He must find the missing girl.

'Where's Miss Peterson? Have they taken her?'

The coachman answered him. 'No, sir. She's somewhere behind us but two men have gone off to look for her.'

They could not be in the lane, he had just galloped through it. Somehow the girl must have got into the field. There was a gap in the hedge. He would take Brutus through. With luck, he could approach them unobserved. He pushed his mount through the confusion of clothes and books and into the field at the far side of the hedge.

He pushed Brutus forward, guiding him with his knees and the reins knotted on the withers. His sword was gripped in his right hand, his pistol loaded and ready in his left. He reached the turn in the road. His hands clenched. He heard the girl's voice

'Here, you may have my purse. There are several guineas in it. I've nothing else of value.'

A coarse voice answered. 'Thank you kindly, miss but it ain't coins we're looking for. We reckon that it's you what we seek.'

Simon kicked hard and the massive gelding almost catapulted him from the saddle as the animal responded. He roared a challenge: often noise would distract an opponent as much as a weapon. The girl reacted instantly, flinging herself sideways and putting the bulk of her horse between herself and her attackers. The two men took to their heels and fled.

Devereux and Dawkins could not be far behind with their troop. Their job was to apprehend those two. His job was done. His head was filled with a strange buzzing, his eyes blurred and then he was falling into a deep pit of blackness.

Lydia saw the colonel slump forward in his saddle. The poor man should not be out of bed, let alone charging across the countryside saving her life. She must take care of him. She ran to his side moments before he toppled to the ground. Talking quietly to Brutus, she guided the animal back through the field toward the voices calling out to her.

'I am safe, but Colonel Westcott has collapsed.'

He was too unwell to remain upright. The only way to get him safely to Bracken Hall was inside the damaged carriage. The debris was swept from the floor of the vehicle and Billy and Fred removed their capes and laid them inside. Sam Smith propped himself against the door and the injured man was laid across his knees. This wasn't ideal, but the best that could be achieved in the circumstances.

'Tom, we must get to the hall as soon as we can. Fred, take Smith's mount, ride ahead and warn Mr Peterson to expect us. Dr Andrews must be sent for immediately.'

No-one questioned her authority. The hastily repacked trunk was strapped for a third time in the luggage space at the rear of the carriage and they were ready to leave.

'This is a rum do, miss. I ain't never seen the like. How comes the colonel and those other two turned up like this and why should the military be coming here?'

She shook her head. 'I've no idea, Billy. But I'm sure someone will arrive to explain it all. My interest in the matter is the health of Colonel Wescott. He should never have left London.'

Under Siege

When Lydia arrived at Bracken Hall, she found two stable hands at the ready, a trestle between them in order to carry the colonel inside. Billy and Fred returned from the yard and were waiting to offer whatever assistance was needed.

'David, has someone been sent to fetch Dr Andrews? Colonel Wescott suffered a severe concussion yesterday morning. The London doctor told him to remain in bed for three days at least. I cannot think what possessed him to gallop about the countryside in this way.'

Sam backed out of the carriage. 'It's like this, Miss Peterson. He knew you was in danger and set out at once. That's the colonel all over, act first and worry about the consequences later.'

It took all four men to move the

injured man from the floor of the carriage to the trestle. With further heaving and grunting, the stretcher bearers staggered to their feet and headed inside. It was perfectly plain they would never get him upstairs. There was no choice, he'd have to go in her father's disused apartment. Goodness knows what sort of state that was in, but it was on the ground floor and would be far easier to access.

The housekeeper, Dorcas Jones, and two parlour-maids were hovering anxiously in the hall.

'Dorcas, we shall use the rooms downstairs. Get one of the girls to fetch clean linen and strip the bed.' She turned to her brother who was supporting the injured man's head. 'You'll have to lay him down on the dining table until his chamber is ready. It's the only place where we have an item of furniture long enough to accommodate him.'

There was no butler at Bracken Hall. She and her brother preferred to live simply. All staff were referred to by their given names and both David and she would not ask the servants to do any task they were not prepared to do themselves, however unpleasant it might be.

She ran ahead to the dining-room. This room was rarely in use, being far too grand for just David and herself. The trestle would scratch the polished surface disastrously, so she needed a cover of some sort. Tablecloths? Yes, there was a stack of damask in the sideboard. Snatching several, she tossed them across the table just as the four men staggered in, red-faced and sweating.

'Put Colonel Wescott here for the moment. Sam, will you take care of him until his room is ready?'

'He'll do fine on here. He's slept in far worse places on campaign abroad.'

The maids had already made the bed and one of them was running a warming pan back and forth across the mattress. The bed had not been slept in for many years, but the room was dry.

The bed was ready, the pillows plumped, covers removed and the furniture given a quick dust before the clock struck the hour. Lydia checked the room to make sure everything was as it should be. There was a basin of warm water, bandages, scissors and a nightshirt of her brother's. It would be broad enough, but far too short. Never mind.

'Carefully does it, lads. Back a little, swing round. There now straight ahead.' Following David's instructions, the men, coughing and grunting, brought in the patient. 'Hold the trestle steady, we need to transfer him to the bed.'

With David supporting the patient's head and shoulders and Lydia, the housekeeper and the two parlourmaids holding the rest of his body, the colonel was rolled into the waiting bed.

'Excellent work, Sam Smith. I shall leave you and Mr Peterson to disrobe him. I must go down to the stables and check on Black Bess.'

David's voice followed her from the

room. 'The mare's neither eaten nor drunk since yesterday. If she doesn't do so soon we will lose the foal.'

Martha was waiting for her at the bottom of the stairs. 'Do you need me, Miss Peterson? Shall I see what I can do about salvaging some of your garments?'

'Please do that, Martha. I'm going to the stables. I shall need something to eat when I return.' Martha stared pointedly at her velvet habit. 'I know, but I don't have time to change. There's been far too much delay already.' Dorcas, who was nearby, bustled off to the kitchen to inform Cook that dinner would be needed early today.

Normally when she was at home, she ate a hearty breakfast and then nothing until she dined, around four o'clock most days. Then, if she was still hungry, she took supper around nine o'clock. David followed her lead.

Her lips curved. Perhaps she'd spent too long with gentlemen who always did her bidding. Could this be why she and Colonel Westcott were always at odds?

She shivered as she stepped outside. Now was not the time to think of such things. The sun had gone behind a second bank of ominous clouds.

'Billy, I think there might be another of those storms approaching. We cannot leave Jenkins where he is. The likelihood of a troop of militia just happening to pass by is absurd. There's something about all this that escapes me.'

'It's a havey-cavey business indeed, miss. I've already taken the liberty of sending the diligence out, seeing as you and the master were somewhat occupied inside. Fred and three stout lads have gone. They're armed and ready for trouble. They should be back before dark with the prisoners and Jenkins. That's if he's not been spirited away by the military.'

'The prisoners must go in the cellar underneath the clock tower. It's fortunate the tower is the other side of the yard, well away from the main building.

Have water, food, blankets and palliasses taken down.'

Having these footpads incarcerated so close to the house was unfortunate, but she had no choice. They must be held until they were taken away by a higher authority. Jenkins would understand the correct procedure, he'd been a soldier himself.

Black Bess was nipping at her distended belly, shaking her head and stamping every few moments. Something was definitely amiss.

'Easy, Bess, I'm here now. What's wrong, girl? It's too soon for you to foal.'

The mare raised her head, her eyes were dull, her coat sweat-stained. The sooner she got the animal comfortable and persuaded her to drink, the better. She was so engrossed in her task she forgot about the man lying desperately ill in the house. She didn't leave the loose box until Bess had drunk a pail of fresh water and eaten a warm bran mash. It had taken her time to achieve her objective, but eventually she was sure the mare was out of danger.

Billy had been assisting her. He rubbed his eyes. 'Shall I rug her up again? The wind's bitter and it's raining heavily.'

She straightened, leaning tiredly against the stable wall. 'Yes, do that, Billy. We have eased the foal into a more comfortable position.'

It was quite dark outside. The lanterns were swinging crazily, making the light dance. Only then, she remembered Colonel Wescott. How was he doing? Had the doctor been able to revive him? The lashing rain made it impossible to converse outside. She took to her heels and raced for the rear door; time enough to ask questions when she was safe inside.

She was soaked to the skin, her riding habit beyond repair, but she must change before inquiring about the patient. Had Jenkins returned and were the unwanted guests safely locked in a cellar?

Using the back stairs, as she always

did when she returned from the yard, she emerged in her own apartment through the servants' entrance.

'There you are, miss. You must be that tired and hungry. My word, I think your habit's fit only for the ragbag.'

'I know, most unfortunate. Martha, tell me please, what news of the patient?'

Whilst soaking in a hot bath, her maid gave her welcome news. The colonel was still with them. The soldiers hadn't appeared to collect the prisoners and Jenkins had been delighted to return in the diligence with her men.

With her hair dripping, she sat up. 'I'm done here, Martha. Kindly hand me a towel for my hair. I'm fully restored, but ravenous.'

She rose gracefully from the water, but almost slipped at Martha's gasp.

'My word, miss, you're black and blue. I'd no idea you'd taken such a bad fall yesterday.'

She dressed quickly and discovered David waiting for her in the passage-way, his dark hair in disarray.

'Good, I was about to come up and see you. You must be famished, I told them to serve dinner immediately. Let's go through, I'll tell you everything I know about the colonel's health. I also must tell you what Jenkins said about the matter.'

After two bowls of leek and potato soup, a generous portion of steak and kidney pudding followed by fruit, nuts and plum cake, Lydia felt herself ready for conversation.

'I've no idea what all this is about, David, and until the colonel recovers his senses I feel we shall not discover the whole. Jenkins and Smith are as much in the dark as we are.'

'They knew you were in grave danger from an attack, but Westcott failed to enlighten them as to who would be doing the attacking or how he came to have this knowledge.'

She pushed back her chair, almost too full to move. 'I'm going along to see how Colonel Wescott is. He saved my life, he's a brave and resourceful man, but foolhardy in the extreme. But first I must tell you everything that has happened in the last two days.'

When she'd finished the story, her brother shook his head in bewilderment.

'None of this makes any sense. However, when the coach fails to return tomorrow, Edward will no doubt eventually send someone to investigate.'

'And by a stroke of misfortune I've now ruined two carriages. Ellen is quite right to say that calamity and I are companions.'

'And by the by, you cannot visit Wescott in his bedchamber even if he is unconscious. That will never do.'

'I know that. I shall speak to him when he's recovered.' She pursed her lips. 'How stupid of me. Of course, I must write to Edward. Whatever's going on, he has to be a party to it. We must send someone to London tomorrow morning. We should have the information we require before supper. Edward must know why those men were chasing me. I don't wish to wait until

Westcott recovers his senses to discover what all this is about. It could be several days before he is able to speak to us.'

'With luck, the coach will be fully restored by the time Edward appears. I have two men instructed to work on it through the night.'

'I doubt it will ever be the same. It's most unfortunate. Ellen has not set foot in it and already it's damaged.' She yawned; she ached in every bone. The sooner she found her bed, the better.

The news from the sickroom was unchanged. The patient was still deeply unconscious, but no worse or better than before.

The rain had not abated. The narrow lanes in their vicinity would be a quagmire for several days to come. Perhaps the promised military had been obliged to find shelter and would arrive tomorrow.

She woke a little after midnight, and found herself unable to drift off again. Lydia was not normally given to flights of fancy, but for some reason she'd woken from a dream in which he was in mortal danger. Exactly what kind of danger had not been clear, but she had to put her mind at rest before she could settle.

There was no need to rouse the household. She would take the back stairs and visit the apartment with no-one else the wiser. His valet was bound to be sitting by the bedside; she could attract his attention and ask him how things were without breaching any rules of etiquette. With her indoor slippers on and her thick wrap tied securely, she took a single candlestick and set out.

For some reason, she started at every sound, hesitated in places that were as familiar to her as her own bedchamber. It must be the storm: the wind howling round the house, the rain beating against the windowpanes, that was unsettling her.

Over the past seven years she'd made many journeys in the dead of night to attend to the horses. However on those occasions she was dressed in breeches and boots. Descending the twisting staircase whilst holding on to her skirts with one hand and a candlestick in the other was decidedly difficult. How the servants managed carrying brimming buckets without mishap was nothing short of a marvel. It was high time they used some of their savings to install plumbing.

Squire Bentley had already got a newfangled bathing room. It was the talk of the neighbourhood. The next time his wife invited them to dine she would accept so that she could see this technological wonder for herself.

This part of the house was unfamiliar to her in the dark. An icy blast blew out her candle; now she would have to reach her destination by touching the panels. The entrance to the apartment was not far ahead, so she inched her way along the passage until she felt the wall give beneath her fingers.

Thank goodness, there was a lamp burning in the dressing-room. Not liking to call out in case she disturbed

Westcott, she crept to the bedchamber door and pushed it open.

The hair on the back of her neck stood up. Sam was stretched out on the carpet. Someone had attacked him. There was nothing she could do; she had no weapon. She must slip away and rouse David. He could go to the gun room and arm himself.

As she was sliding backward, a man spoke. She recognised the voice and cold sweat trickled between her shoulder blades. The voice was that of one of the men who'd accosted her earlier. He must have followed the diligence and come in by the French doors. Why hadn't she thought to pull the shutters?

'We'll wake him up. Tip that jug of water over his head. He'll tell us where it is if we threaten to burn the house down. Soldiers will be here first thing; it'll be too late then to recover it. If we want rich pickings, we got to find it tonight.'

She couldn't let them do this, if the colonel were drenched in cold water it might prove fatal. What could she do to save him?

Could she burst in and disable one of the men? No, that would be too dangerous. They would overcome her as well.

She sent up a fervent prayer, asking for guidance.

When she opened her eyes she knew what she must do. She snatched up a candlestick and an enamel basin.

Her heart was pounding; she feared they would hear it in the bedchamber. There was not a minute to lose. She drew a deep breath and stepped out into the bedchamber. She screamed and howled like an inmate of Bedlam whilst hammering the candlestick against the base of the bowl. Her sudden appearance was too much for the intruders who sensed the entire household was about to waken. They dropped the jug on the floor and fled as if the hounds of hell were behind them.

She ran to the windows and slammed them shut, banging the shutters closed as well. She dropped the bar across and slumped to the floor. The racket must have been heard throughout the hall; all she had to do was remain here quietly until David came to take charge.

Then, in the darkness, there was the unmistakable sound of someone moving. Sick with dread, she crouched down, too petrified to stir. There had been a third man in the room. He was locked inside with her and the colonel. However hard she tried, she could not prevent a sob escaping.

★　★　★

Simon was wrenched from his deep sleep by a hideous cacophony. Completely disoriented, for a second he believed he was in Hades. The unearthly screaming, the banging and the sound of pounding footsteps added to his confusion. Where was he? What was that painful din?

The noise stopped abruptly and blessed silence followed. He'd been having a nightmare; he must have imagined the racket. Then lighter feet ran past and the double slam of the windows and shutters echoed through the room. He blinked to clear his eyes. A faint glow came from a dressing-room, enough to see that Sam was unconscious on the carpet. He heard the unmistakable sound of a person by the window and then quiet again.

Forcing himself to his elbows, he waited to see if his head would spin. It ached abominably, but otherwise he was compos mentis. He breathed silently, not wishing to alert whoever it was on the far side of the room.

It was Miss Peterson! She was crying. He could see her crouching against the shutters. His inclination was to go to her side and offer her comfort. But enough rules had been broken by her entering his bedchamber, far better to remain where he was and encourage her by voice alone. What could have possessed her to come in like this?

'My dear Miss Peterson, can you

raise yourself? Sam is in need of your help.'

She scrambled to her feet. 'Thank goodness! I'd no idea you were conscious, sir, I am so relieved. I thought I had shut a third villain in here with us.'

'Villain? What the devil are you talking about?'

'Did you not hear them? The two ruffians who accosted me earlier were in here threatening to hurt you. That's why I made such a din.'

Poor girl; no wonder she had been scared witless. 'I'm impressed by your courage, my dear. I could do with a dozen like you in my brigade. Can you light some candles? I shall remain where I am, but I should be able to judge how bad my man's injuries are when the room is brighter.'

'I shall do so at once. How remiss of me to ignore his plight. There's an oil lamp I can use to do this, I don't believe my hands are sufficiently steady to use the tinderbox.' She appeared, holding a lit candle, and moments later he was able to peer down at Sam. Lydia smiled at him, her head tilted to one side, her amazing green eyes sparkling. 'You have made a remarkable recovery. We thought you at death's door. Well, Dr Andrew certainly did.'

'I was tired, no more than that. Apart from a thumping headache, I'm fully restored.'

'Then you can help me . . . ' Even in the half light, he saw her cheeks turn scarlet.

'Exactly so, my dear. Far better I remain where I am.'

She dropped to her knees, placing her forefingers against Smith's neck. 'His pulse is steady. I think he'll be coming round soon. I'm afraid that he has a lump the size of a pigeon's egg on the back of his head but there is little blood.'

'Leave him where he is, Miss Peterson. You must rouse the house. It's imperative that I speak to your brother. Our lives might well depend on it.'

Lydia's stomach clenched. 'But I have barred the door? Surely that's enough?'

Then she recalled the intruders had been looking for something specific, intending to force the colonel to reveal its whereabouts. No common thief would follow a quarry to their home and break in.

'I shall ring the bell in a moment, but first I demand that you tell me what all this is about. I do not wish to be excluded, and as soon as David arrives I shall have to leave. He is going to think it most improper that I'm here in the first place.'

His eyes narrowed and he stared at her before nodding.

'Very well, I shall give you a brief synopsis. Arthur was struck down by a book, not a stone. This book is of paramount importance to the government but even more so to the traitors who are plotting to rescue Bonaparte from Elba.'

'I knew it. I have seen the book they

seek. Good grief! It's still in the pocket of the riding habit I was wearing, I'd quite forgotten I'd put it there. I told my maid to throw the garment into the ragbag. I shall go at once and retrieve it.'

He didn't detain her, but continued to watch her in the most disconcerting way. Her cheeks coloured for a second time under his scrutiny.

What was it about this man that so unsettled her? She was tugging at the bell strap when she froze.

'Colonel, there's something you do not know. Jenkins brought the prisoners back here. They're locked in a cellar under the clock tower on the other side of the yard. The two men who were in here might find and release them.'

Ignoring her sensibilities, he cursed volubly. Then to her horror, he threw the covers aside and leapt out of bed. She flinched in horror; she'd never seen a gentleman's knees before.

'Go away, Miss Peterson. I must get dressed.'

He had no need to tell her a second time.

She fled from the room, exiting the apartment through the double doors that led into the main part of the house. Why was nobody up? Had she not made sufficient noise to rouse the dead? They needed to barricade themselves in before there were six men trying to enter and steal the precious volume. There was one way she could be certain everyone in the household would get up.

Gathering the skirts of her wrap she raced to the entrance hall. Taking the beater, she hammered on the brass gong and the noise reverberated throughout the house. She was more than ready to hand over responsibility to her brother and the colonel.

David appeared on the stairs, still tucking his nightshirt into his breeches, barefoot with his boots held precariously under one arm. 'What is it? Has the colonel died?'

'No, he's fully recovered. But his man has been hit on the head by two of the thieves that waylaid us earlier. Fortunately, I was able to scare them away. Far worse than that, David, soon there will be six men trying to get in to recover a secret code book. It's imperative that they don't get their hands on it.'

'You take the chambers on the right. I'll take those on the left. Check that the shutters are securely barred.'

He hopped away, dragging his boots on, not waiting to see if she followed his instructions. She should have thought of that herself. However, the sight of the colonel in his nightshirt had quite unnerved her.

By the time she'd rushed from room to room and returned to the entrance hall, the whole house was awake. She shivered. The desperate men outside must also be aware of this.

The colonel looked every inch a soldier. He was barking commands to Jenkins, Fred, Billy and two other stable hands. They were responding with enthusiasm. David was holding his pistols. He was an expert shot, they both were, but seeing weapons drawn inside her house was deeply shocking.

The colonel saw her first. From commanding officer he turned instantly to a charming gentleman. His smile softened his features, and made her feel secure and loved.

Where had that nonsensical idea sprang from?

The candlestick slipped from her fingers to land painfully on her toe. He was at her side in an instant.

'My dear girl, let me see. I hope you haven't broken anything.'

David arrived at her side. 'I think not, Colonel Westcott. Our housekeeper shall attend to my sister. She should not be down here. None of the women should be involved in this matter.'

Tension flickered between the two men. Then the colonel rose smoothly to his feet and nodded. 'I beg your pardon, Miss Peterson. You have done magnificently tonight. I believe I owe my life to you for a second time. But your part is done. Peterson is quite right; you must remain upstairs. Lock yourself into your bedchamber and remain there until this matter is brought to a conclusion.'

Lydia wasn't sure with whom she was more cross. There was no future in arguing the point. Both men were waiting for her to remove herself. She pinned on a false smile. 'Of course, you're both correct. Dorcas, let me take your arm. We are in the way down here.'

The housekeeper, two parlourmaids, two chambermaids and Martha accompanied her into her apartment. No sooner was the door closed behind them than she turned to her maid. 'Help me get dressed. I shall put on my work clothes; breeches and boots are needed tonight, not gowns.'

'But your foot, Miss Peterson? Is it not badly damaged? That candlestick was brass, it could have broken a bone.'

Lydia held up her foot for inspection. 'See? It's bruised but no more than that. Martha, have you taken my riding habit away?'

'No, ma'am, it's still in the linen basket. I reckon there's enough material can be salvaged to make something else. But it needs laundering first.'

Not wishing to explain why her question was so urgent, Lydia hurried into the dressing-room to find the garment. Reaching into the pocket, she was relieved to find the missing book where she'd left it. She hid it in her sleeve just as Martha joined her.

She returned to her bedchamber, hastily tucking the small volume under her pillow as she removed her night clothes.

* * *

Simon watched as Lydia limped away. When all this was sorted, he'd ask Peterson's permission to pay his addresses. In spite of the seriousness of the situation, he was obliged to restrain the urge to clap the young man on the back, to embrace him and call him brother. It was imperative he pushed such feelings to one side and concentrate on the matter in hand.

But it was hard. He'd never been in love before.

His jaw dropped. In love? How could that have happened? Until this moment he thought himself immune to such emotions. From now on he must be vigilant, not just for himself, but for Lydia, the young woman who had become the most precious person in his life.

'Colonel Wescott! Colonel Wescott, are you feeling unwell?'

Simon was jerked back to his duties by Peterson's anxious inquiry. 'I am perfectly well. Has everything been done as I ordered?'

'We now have seven able-bodied men inside with us, all fully armed. The house is barricaded. There's no way to gain entry from the outside. We have sufficient food and water to maintain a siege for two weeks.'

'Good grief, man, it shall not come to that. If it were not for the ladies, I should take the fight to them. Rein-forcements will arrive as soon as the storm abates. All we have to do is remain vigilant until then.'

'There are still two stable hands in the yard. I could not leave our horses unattended. They have strict instruc-tions to keep away from the house and remain hidden from the traitors.'

'Excellent. With luck it will take some time for them to release the prisoners. This heavy rain might well be to our benefit in the end.'

Simon frowned. Thinking about Lydia had made him forget about the most important matter; he'd yet to recover the codebook. Peterson must speak to his sister and discover where it was hidden. To his annoyance, he saw the girl at the head of the stairs. She was dressed in men's attire, her glorious hair hidden under a soft cap and her womanly shape disguised under a loose frockcoat.

Lydia nearly laughed out loud at the colonel's expression. Braving his anger

was worth it just to see him discon-
certed.

'I have what you seek here, Colonel
Wescott.'

His expression icy, the colonel held
out his hand and she placed the book in
it. 'Thank you, Miss Peterson. I would
like to speak to you privately, kindly
come with me.'

She glanced at David, but he
shrugged and gestured for her to follow
the colonel into the drawing-room. Her
heart was beating rapidly. Why did this
man cause her to lose her courage? This
would not do.

She stiffened her spine, tossing her
head and unaware that her cap had
slipped askew. She would not be put off
by his anger; she had as much right as
anyone to be in the midst of the action.
She could handle a gun as well as any
man and was quite capable of putting a
bullet in a traitor if the safety of her
country should depend upon it.

Halting two yards from him, she
glared right back. Something flickered

in his eyes and the rigidity in his jaw released. Surely it was not amusement she detected in his expression? Her knees threatened to give way and she flopped into a dilapidated armchair. He grabbed a chair, swinging it round to straddle it, then folding his arms across the back, he rested his chin on his hands and sighed.

'You are impossible, my dear. I've never met anyone like you. There is no other of my acquaintance who would think to disobey my orders.' He sounded more resigned than angry.

'I do beg your pardon, Colonel Wescott. However, I am no green girl, and, as you must be quite aware, have been running this household since my father's demise five years ago.' She paused, staring at him suspiciously. 'I have also been running the business with my brother since that time. Although legally I have no rights, in fact it is I who am in command here. Edward is nominally the head of the household but he does not interfere.'

His eyes crinkled endearingly at the corners and his smile diffused her anger. 'That does not surprise me one jot, my dear. You're a formidable woman but I must ask you to follow my instructions in this matter. I am the soldier, it's my job to command and keep those close to me safe from harm.'

She couldn't resist. Her antagonism melted. 'I would not have that precious book in the hands of traitors. I might be a woman, but I'm prepared to give my life for my country as any man might do.'

His hand came out and she stilled. Was he going to touch her face? But all he did was gently pull her cap straight, no wonder he'd been smiling at her.

'I'm sure you are, my dear. However, it's entirely unnecessary. There are nine of us and only six of them. A troop of highly trained soldiers will be here tomorrow. All we have to do is remain inside and wait.'

'Very well, I shall do as you bid. I have no wish to cause any extra difficulties. However, I shall take my pistols upstairs and remain alert. I shall consider it my duty to protect the women waiting with me.

He stood up, tossing the chair to one side as if it weighed nothing. 'It's going to be a long night.'

A House In Peril

Lydia returned to her chambers, knowing she would get no further rest that night. She would remain awake and let the youngest members of staff use her bedroom. Good heavens! Cook was still upstairs in her chamber; she must send the maids to fetch her.

Simon was in the master suite that faced the front of the house. Although the shutters were closed, he'd left a gap to reconnoitre the surrounding area.

David spoke from behind him. 'It's near impossible to hear anything outside. The rain's drowning out everything else and it's too dark to see.'

'I've seen no lights and no sign of activity in the region of the clock tower. However, those men must have released the others by now. Perhaps they're sheltering inside, waiting for us to become less vigilant.' He gestured to Jenkins to join him. 'You take this window. Keep your rifle trained on the clock tower. Any movement there, fire but don't shoot to kill unless you have no choice. I'm sure the military would prefer to take these men alive. They have valuable information.'

Simon thought he would check on Lydia. His mouth curved; she was no longer Miss Peterson to him, but Lydia, the woman he loved. He must be certain the door was securely bolted from the inside, that they had drawn the shutters and pushed items of furniture across all entrances.

The entire house was fully lit as if for a grand party, candles blazing in their sconces and every oil lamp burning. He wanted the men outside to understand they were expected, that attempting to break in could well prove fatal.

He knocked sharply on the door of Lydia's apartment. There was a pause and then someone spoke from behind it.

'Who is it? Kindly identify yourself.'

'It is I, Westcott. Has everything been done as I instructed?'

'Yes, sir. We are secure in here.'

'Excellent. I bid you good night. You have nothing with which to concern yourselves. Everything is in hand here and the house fully protected.'

As he retraced his steps he wondered why Lydia hadn't come to speak to him herself. He would go back and ask her to come out. He shrugged; no doubt she was still annoyed with him for sending her upstairs. He did not wish to have unresolved animosity between them. He strode back to the door and rapped a second time.

'Miss Peterson, I should like to speak to you most urgently.'

There was the sound of something heavy being moved and the key turned. She appeared in the doorway. 'You cannot come in here, sir. It would be most unseemly.'

Simon had no intention of holding

this conversation with half a dozen members of her staff eavesdropping. Before she could protest, he took her hand and pulled her into the corridor. 'We can sit on the window seat, my dear, it will be perfectly proper, but we shall be private.'

He ushered her to the window seat and watched her curl up with her feet beneath her. A slight smile played around his mouth.

'There are one or two things I would like clarified. How did you come to be downstairs in my bedchamber in your night attire?'

How could he be so indelicate as to ask her this? With fiery cheeks and lowered lashes, she mumbled her reply. 'I had a nightmare which woke me up and for some reason I felt that you were in danger. I could not settle until I'd been down to discover for myself how you were. I had no intention of coming into your chamber. I was going to speak to Smith through the dressing-room door. There would have been no breach of etiquette.' She risked a shy glance at her inquisitor.

'And I'm grateful that you did, my dear.' He stretched out his long legs and smiled at her. His eyes were gentle, his expression loving. 'Do you get the feeling our lives are inextricably linked, sweetheart? That a force greater than ourselves has brought us together to the benefit of both?'

'Good gracious! How can that be? We were at daggers drawn for the first ten days of our acquaintance.'

He leant forward. 'I rather think that was because we are so similar. I changed my opinion two days ago, after the riding accident. I was rather hoping you had come to see me in a different light.'

He reached out and captured her hands. Hers were lost inside his clasp. His skin felt rough and calloused, hers far softer. She had no wish to snatch them back and felt comforted by his closeness.

'I have, Colonel, I believe that you

could become a dear friend.'

His fingers tightened. 'I would like to be more that, but now is not the time or the place to talk of it. When this is over, my dear, I intend to ask you a very particular question. Do you think you might give me an answer in the affirmative?'

He was going to make her an offer. Did she want to marry a soldier? It would mean leaving her beloved horses, following the drum. Such a marriage was not something she could contemplate without serious consideration. Gently she withdrew her hands and smiled. 'I'm not sure, sir, but I promise I shall give the matter a deal of thought. That is the best I can say at the moment.'

He nodded as if satisfied with her answer. 'I can ask for no more. I must return to France when my leave is finished. It might be several months before I return. You can give me your answer then.'

Several months? The thought of not

seeing him for so long caused words to tumble from her lips of their own volition. 'I shall give you my answer tomorrow. I would not dream of sending you away without one.'

His smile bathed her in a warm glow of happiness. She knew already what her answer would be. If she had a choice between travelling around the continent like a gypsy or remaining at home without him, there was no question that her reply would be yes.

He stood up and offered his hand. She took it and he pulled her to her feet. 'Go back in, sweetheart.'

She almost skipped back to her room. She was all but betrothed to the colonel. If she married him what a tangle the relationships would be. Would Ellen now become her sister-in-law as well as her sister? She was still laughing at her nonsense as she locked the door behind her.

She was surprised to see the young maids sitting on one of the day beds. Why weren't they resting as instructed by the housekeeper?

'Miss Peterson,' Dorcas said anxiously. 'The girls are reluctant to retire. They have been quite overwhelmed by the excitement. The thought that a band of renegades might attack the house has made them nervous and they cannot settle.'

Lydia might have mass hysteria to contend with if she didn't find something to distract them. 'I think what we all need is a hot drink and something to eat before we go to bed.'

Immediately they forgot their fears and were happy to accompany her downstairs. Lydia was well aware that if she was discovered she would be in serious trouble. It was up to her to keep everyone calm and happy. There could be no danger in taking the back stairs and going into the kitchen.

'We must be very quiet. We do not wish to alert any of the gentleman. If they know what we're about they might insist we make refreshments for them as well.' This seemed a safe alternative to the truth. Without the usual chatter and clatter, the four of them descended the back stairs and crept into the kitchen.

Here they were relaxed; this was their normal environment. Lydia sat quietly at the table and waited for them to swing the kettle over the flames.

Her heart pounded every time she heard a noise. She was sure there was someone in the corridor. By the time the two trays were laden, she was thoroughly agitated.

'Dorcas, we must make haste, I'm sure I heard someone outside. I do not wish to be discovered down here.'

The housekeeper nodded. 'We're done here, miss. Betty and Sally can carry the trays. Will you be able to bank down the range before you leave?'

'Of course I will, Dorcas. You go ahead. I shall be with you directly.'

Her task completed and all but her own candle doused, she was ready to depart. Her hand was on the kitchen door when she heard the unmistakable sound of stealthy footsteps approaching.

The door opened.

She froze. Her eyes widened and the candlestick slipped from her fingers.

★ ★ ★

The library had become Simon's headquarters. He paced the carpet. Something was amiss; his instincts told him so. Why hadn't the men attacked? It didn't make sense they must know their time was limited. Peterson was stretched out on a sofa. He didn't have the heart to rouse him. He'd go round and check with the other men.

It would be dawn in a couple of hours, the attempt to break in must come soon. Jenkins was at his post, his rifle barrel resting on the balustrade of the small balcony that ran outside the windows.

He was halfway down the main staircase when a door opened behind him. He was running when the housekeeper rushed out to greet him, her face etched with concern.

'Thank heavens. I was coming to fetch you, sir. We went downstairs to make ourselves tea. Miss Peterson was right behind us. She just had to tend to the fire. I was halfway up the staircase when I heard noises in the passageway. Something's happened to her. Those men are inside the house and have taken her!'

Sam had been correct. Simon bit back a mouthful of curses — better not to offend the lady if he could avoid it.

'Remain where you are, madam. I shall go and investigate. Is there any way you can secure the door that leads to the back stairs?'

'There is, sir. The door opens inwards. We can push a set of drawers across.'

'Excellent. Do so at once. Whatever happens, stay put.'

What in tarnation had made the girl disobey his orders again? The commotion had brought Jenkins out from the front room.

'They're in the house, Jenkins. Fetch the others and bring them to me. They've taken Miss Peterson hostage.'

Her brother was on his feet when he strode into the library. 'Peterson, the beggars have got in. They've captured your sister.'

'They've got Lydia? How did they get into her chamber? I can't understand why we didn't hear them.'

'They didn't get upstairs. She accompanied the housekeeper to the kitchen and must have come face to face with them in the servants' quarters.'

'The coal hatch! They must have come in that way. I didn't think to lock that earlier. This is all my fault. What a disaster.'

'Enough of that. I need you to have a cool head and we must plan our strategy.'

'You will have to give them the book. They will trade her for it I am sure.'

Simon shook his head. The young man didn't understand the gravity of the situation. Whatever his personal feelings on the matter, the safety of the book was paramount. 'Handing over the book is not an option.'

Peterson swung towards him, his face ravaged with grief and his fists clenched. Simon raised a hand in warning.

'Although I cannot give up the volume, I give you my word your sister shall come to no harm. I must think. There has to be a way we can save her life and not betray our country.'

★ ★ ★

Lydia clutched the table edge for support. Confronting her was a rough, unshaven man, his garments covered in coal dust, his broken teeth bared in a smile. She should scream to alert the house. As she drew breath to raise the alarm the man surged forward. 'Make a sound and yer dead, missy,' he whispered.

Two more villains slipped into the kitchen. Without a word being spoken, she was trussed and a rag stuffed in her mouth. There was nothing she could do. Her disobedience had cost her dear. A stinking individual grabbed her and slung her over his shoulder as if she was a sack of potatoes.

Where were they taking her? The rank smell and the clouds of coal dust filling her nose was making her stomach heave.

From her upside down position, she was aware that there were at least three or four accomplices in the passageway. If Simon knew the men were inside they would have the advantage of number. She was dumped unceremoni-ously against the wall in the servants' hall, her head striking painfully on the side of the long bureau in which the cutlery and crockery were stored.

The leader of the gang turned the key and gestured to his henchmen to push the heavy oak table against the door. Then one produced a tinderbox and lit several candles. The candlelight con-firmed what she feared. Her captors were armed to the teeth.

Had they forgotten she was there? Their inattention gave her the time to study the group in more detail. Perhaps one amongst them was not as evil as the rest, one that might be persuaded to help her.

The leader had a decisiveness of purpose and implacability that told her he would slit her throat in a second if she gave him cause. It would be more prudent to wait for Simon to come for her, but she intended to look for a way of freeing herself. The leader spoke. His voice was little above a whisper, but she could hear his words quite clearly.

'Luck's on our side tonight, boys. First we found the coal hole unbolted and then we got ourselves a bargaining tool. Someone will come looking for this one; she'll be missed soon enough. I reckon that tall dark one, the one that's supposed to be sick in bed, will be happy to give us the book in return for her life.'

'I'm sure he will. We ain't going to have to fetch him. We'll sit tight until he comes to us. I reckon we'll come out of this all right.'

A voice she recognised spoke up next. 'Why's she dressed like that? You reckon they need the women to fight us?'

Someone was standing next to her. The leader wrenched the cloth from her mouth. 'Tell me, how many men are there? Do you know where the book is?'

She was tempted to defy him, to refuse to answer, but that would do nothing to help the situation. 'Colonel Sinclair has eight men, two of them marksmen and they have their rifles with them. All the rest are armed as well.' Her voice wobbled and she forced herself to sound more confident. 'I have no idea what book you're speaking of.'

His lips curled back in a smile that did not reach his eyes. 'You'd better hope he has the book, missy, or you'll not see another sunrise.'

The cloth was stuffed back between her teeth and the ruffian laughed and turned away as if she was of no account. This was all her fault.

Colonel Wescott would never part with the book, he was a soldier, his duty must come first.

Her eyes filled. She wished she'd had the opportunity to tell Simon that she loved him. In spite of the dire circumstances she felt a swell of happiness. She was almost certain he felt the same about her.

★ ★ ★

Simon had faced worse odds many times and triumphed, but this situation was not like any other. Tonight he must think of a way to do his duty and also save the woman he loved. He paced the carpet in the library. Having his emotions involved made it impossible to be analytical.

Then inspiration came to him. He knew exactly what he had to do.

David was glaring at him from the far side of the room.

'We have one chance, but I need time

to pull it off. Do you have a book of sermons on your shelves? It must have a black cover and look similar to this.' He flicked open the pages to show David. 'See, the letters are ringed in a distinct order. It's a code of some sort. These men will be illiterate; no doubt one book will look very much another to them.'

'Draw random circles then hand them the substitute? That's a capital notion.' The young man flung himself at the book lined walls, frantically scrabbling through a section until he pulled a volume out. 'This is the exact same volume of sermons. I knew the title looked familiar when you showed it to me.'

Simon's shout of delight echoed round the room, bringing Jenkins and Sam to the door to investigate. 'Jenkins, have you secured doors from the lower quarters as I requested?'

'I have, sir, and they are guarded as well.'

He waited until he was alone with

young Peterson. 'In order to complete this task, I must buy you some time. I shall go to them, pretend I'm considering their proposition and demand they give me half an hour. I shall take Jenkins and Sam with me.' He strode to the door, turning back to gesture at the desk. 'Get started, Peterson. Between us we might just pull this off.'

Simon's two men were waiting in the hall, rifles at the ready. 'Come with me, Jenkins, Smith. I'm going to try to negotiate.'

His head was clear, his hands steady he was once more in command of the situation and had his unruly emotions under control. He carried a lantern, his men carried loaded rifles. The passageway was deserted, but he could see light flickering behind the high windows of the servants' hall. He hammered on the door. It was flung open by a rough individual.

'You cannot escape, I have rifles trained on you. The soldiers will be here in a couple of hours. Surrender or die.'

'We have the girl, you have the book. Fair exchange, give it to us and we'll leave. No-one will be harmed. Why have the little lady damaged for the sake of a book that ain't no use to you?'

'I cannot give you the book. It's government property. It is my duty to protect it at all costs.'

The man gestured. Simon heard scrabbling feet and then Lydia cried out in pain. She was dragged forward, tied hand and foot with a filthy rag rammed into her mouth. But her eyes blazed back at him and she shook her head vigorously.

'You are surrounded. I demand that you hand over Miss Peterson.'

'You ain't in no position to make demands. You give me that book or I'll slit her throat.'

'If you release the girl I shall let you and your men leave unharmed. That's the best I can offer.'

'The girl dies unless you bring the book.'

'I need time to decide, I have never betrayed my country.'

The man stared at him for a minute, then he nodded. 'You got half an hour. Be back with the book or your fancy woman will be dead.'

Simon backed away from the room, not trusting the villains not to open fire on him.

'Jenkins, Sam, come with me. We'll be going back with the book.'

In the library, Peterson raised his head and a faint smile flickered across his drawn features. 'Another fifteen minutes, no more, and it'll be done.'

'Good man, I'll leave you to finish. I'm expecting Dawkins and his troop to be here within the hour. Now the rain's stopped . . .'

'They'll not be here that soon, Colonel. The roads will be impassable and the ford flooded; they must make a detour of fifteen miles to the bridge. We can't expect help for several hours.'

'Then we shall have to make this substitution work. If those villains get away, then so be it. They will take nothing of value with them.'

What he hadn't yet told the young man was that it was inevitable they would all be taken prisoner. Lydia would not be exchanged. The men would be forced to give up their weapons, then the rest of his group would be rounded up.

Jenkins said it for him. 'Shall I warn the others to surrender, sir? No point in anyone being hurt.'

To his surprise, Peterson grinned. 'Don't worry, I'd already surmised that's how it would go. You're banking on the traitors being happy with the book, aren't you?'

'I am. With luck, they'll not have discovered the two stable hands hiding in the yard. With luck they can release us when the coast is clear.'

'And if they've been captured?'

'Then we shall have to remain incarcerated until Dawkins and his troop arrive. It's a small inconvenience compared to what could happen.'

★ ★ ★

The gang threw Lydia back into her corner. Her heart was pounding and her mouth dry; if she was to escape she had to do it immediately. Simon had decided to give up the book. She saw it in his eyes.

There were knives stored in the cupboard. There must be some way to get into it.

With one at her disposal, surely she could cut her bonds? It was a remote possibility, but the only idea she had. Far better to fight than remain cowering in a corner. She sighed loudly and slipped down the wall, pretending to swoon.

The men were gathered around the table talking urgently. Now was her opportunity. She toppled sideways so that she was resting with her head beneath the bureau.

Had they heard her? Was someone watching her every move?

It was too dangerous to open her eyes that would reveal she was dissembling and her chance would be lost.

Forcing herself to breathe deeply and evenly, she slumped further until she could feel the edge of the cupboard door beneath her cheek. This was the difficult part; she must nudge it open with her nose without arousing suspicion.

The leader was becoming impatient. 'I'll give him another ten minutes. If he ain't back by then we'll take the girl and go and find him. He'll hand it over soon enough if I stick my knife in his little lady.'

'And then what, guv?'

'Then we'll recover the book and tie the others up. We ain't got time to search for the rest of the staff. I want you two to set a fire under the stairs and burn this place down. We want no witnesses left behind to identify us.'

They were going to murder everyone. It was one thing for her to give up her life for King and country but she could not sit by and let innocent people die as well. She had to make her move immediately.

* * *

The men were occupied, checking their weapons, preparing to spring an ambush on Simon and his men when he returned in good faith to exchange her for the book. She was ignored for the moment.

Slowly, the cupboard door opened an inch or two. She nudged it again until she could see inside. There was a broken knife in the tray on the bottom shelf; this would be better than nothing. How was she to remove it with not even her teeth to assist her?

She eased up until her head and shoulders were inside the cupboard. Any moment she expected to be struck down from behind. Using her chin, somehow she fumbled the knife out. Balanced on the edge of the tray, it fell bouncing against her chest to land between her knees.

Her elation made her incautious, made her forget she was supposed to be asleep. From nowhere, rough hands gripped her shoulders and hauled her backwards.

'You'll not try nothing a second time,' a voice snarled in her ear.

★ ★ ★

'Are we ready, men?' Simon asked. The group murmured their agreement and all but Jenkins and Smith shuffled nervously. 'You stay here, David. Anything goes wrong, guard the real book with your life. Put it back on the shelf. You must never reveal its whereabouts.'

Peterson clasped his hand. 'Save Lydia. She's the world to me.'

On impulse, Simon threw his arm around the young man's shoulders. 'And to me, my boy, and to me. When this is over, I intend to marry your sister.' He grinned. 'I take it I have your permission? Although by rights it is Edward I should apply to. Is he not your guardian?'

'In name only. We send him any

paperwork and his man of business attends to it. Anyway, Lydia does as she pleases. You don't need my permission, but you have my approval. I knew as soon as I met you, you're the man for her.'

Leaving the young man to hide the book, Simon strode out. He was taking only his own men with him. He addressed the others. 'I've decided to give them the book. I believe there's an excellent chance they will be caught before they can hand it on. I cannot sacrifice Miss Peterson.'

A round of approval greeted this remark. No-one, apart from David, knew there had been a substitution.

The barricade was removed. Billy and Fred had instructions to replace the furniture, leaving all the doors available to the intruders. Simon prayed that offering no resistance would save the men's lives. He returned to the servants' quarters, making sure he could be heard. He shouted through the closed door. 'I have the book, I wish to exchange it for Miss Peterson.'

Two rifles and his pistols were trained on the door. The same filthy individual peered through the door.

'You ain't having the girl until you disarm. Drop your weapons and we'll hand her over.'

Simon peered over their heads. Lydia was lying in a crumpled heap, apparently unconscious. Icy rage engulfed him. He removed the book from his pocket and waved it in the air above a flickering sconce. 'If you do not give me Miss Peterson, I shall drop the book in here.'

It was a risk. He would lay down his life for her but they must not know. Two villains picked her up between them. Her head flopped, blood trickling down the side of her face.

Simon didn't hesitate. Enough was enough. 'Put your weapons down, men. It's over. I cannot risk Miss Peterson.'

He dropped his pistol and the others followed suit. No sooner were the weapons on the ground than they were surrounded and bundled into the hall. The book was snatched from his fingers. The man gave it a cursory glance before ramming it in his waistcoat pocket.

Simon was shoved into a chair and tied up by two of the men. The rest of the gang was sent to round up the others.

Five minutes later they were bundled in, trussed and dropped against the far wall. Simon held his breath. His subterfuge had worked. The leaders seemed more intent on getting away than murdering his captives. The door was locked from the outside and they took the candles with them, leaving the room in total darkness.

Simon waited until he was certain they had gone before he made a move. First he must attempt to spit out his gag so he could communicate with the others. It might be possible for one man to release his neighbour.

He must remain calm. There was no immediate urgency to escape from the hall; the danger was past.

But how would the soldiers get in? The house was locked tight. Would they think to try the coal hatch? Had the gang the intelligence to bolt the trap door before they departed? All this could be left until later. He must deal with the situation here.

He'd memorised the room before it had been plunged into darkness. Sam and Jenkins were tied to chairs on the far side of the table. David and the other men were against the wall under the window. But far more important, Lydia was lying directly behind him. How bad were her injuries? If anything were to happen to her, he would not wish to go on living.

He started to throw his weight from side to side until he had gained momentum and then toppled his chair backwards on to the flagstones with an almighty crash. The back splintered. His hands were free.

'I'm free. Everyone remain where you are. I'm going to release Miss Peterson first.'

A series of thumps and grunts told him he was understood. He dropped to his knees and began to edge forward until his fingers touched her. 'Sweetheart, lie still, I'll have you safe directly.' Her skin was warm to the touch, she could not be badly hurt.

He ran his hands down her body and something sharp nicked his finger. He swore and lifted out the object that had injured him, the blade of a sharp knife. Excellent, this was going to make removing the ropes from her hands and feet far easier. By touch he gently pulled the gag over her head.

A rush of relief poured through him as she stirred and mumbled something. 'I must undo the men, my love, but will be back to you as soon as I've done so.'

He stood up, keeping his eyes closed it was far easier to negotiate in darkness when you weren't trying to see. He took one stride to the table. He would release Jenkins then his man could do the rest. This wasn't the first time they'd found themselves in such a predicament.

When he removed his gag Jenkins coughed and cleared his throat noisily. 'You take care of Miss Peterson, sir. Leave this to me.'

Someone attempted to speak whilst kicking the floor. David was trying to attract his attention. Leaving Jenkins to release Sam, he dropped to his knees and made his way carefully across the room.

'David, bang your feet so I can find you more easily.'

A series of thumps directed him to the left. With outstretched hands, he edged forward until his knees bumped into the person he was seeking. Immediately he snatched the gag from David's mouth. 'Young man, do you know where there're candles and a tinderbox?'

'They're stored in a cupboard next to the fireplace. Have you seen to Lydia yet?'

'He has no need do to anything for

me, David. I'm a trifle dizzy, but otherwise unhurt. I'm going to stand up and get out of everyone's way.'

Simon grasped the young man's hands. He knew David was equally relieved the young woman they both loved was conscious. She laughed softly in the darkness.

Although Lydia had told Simon she was fine, her thoughts were jumbled, the pain in her head making it difficult to concentrate. Once the room was lit, she'd take the opportunity to sit and rest. Crashing and voices in the darkness indicated the other men were free and blundering about the pitch black room. She and David had the advantage. Although they didn't visit the servants' hall that often they knew its layout well enough.

As she knelt by the cupboard, she hesitated. There was something she should be telling Simon but she couldn't recall what it was.

Her outstretched fingers found the door latch and she pulled it open.

Reaching in, she soon located the tinderbox and two candles. Simon arrived at her side. She knew instinctively it was him without him having to speak. His arms slipped round her waist and he gathered her gently against his chest. She relaxed into his embrace, feeling safe for the first time that night.

'Do you have the candles, my love?' He didn't release her. No-one could see he was doing anything improper.

'I do, but I have not yet discovered any candlesticks. Once we have some light no doubt we'll find some easily enough.'

Slowly she rotated within his grip, stepping away before placing the candles and tinderbox in his outstretched hands. To her surprise, he was able to turn and toss the objects on to the table. Could he see in the dark? Then his arms were around her once more. His voice was soft in her hair.

David spoke from the darkness. 'Have you found the candles, Lydia? We're standing around here afraid to move in case we trip over something.'

She stepped away from Simon and moved cautiously to the table before answering. 'I'm going to try and light one this very minute.' She picked up the tinderbox but had difficulty locating the aperture.

'Let me do it, Lydia. Your hands will not be steady enough to strike a light.'

Simon succeeded and the first candles were alight. It was a relief to be able to see once more. She was about to pass him the bundle when her eyes widened, his shape became blurred and she feared she would swoon. She'd finally recalled what had been niggling at the back of the brain, the vital information she'd overheard.

Stumbling forward into his outstretched arms, she was hardly able to form the words. 'Simon, they have set fire to the house. They intend all of us to perish in the blaze. I'm so sorry, I should have told you immediately.'

'Are you sure? The air is clear enough in here. If they set it before they left I'm sure we would be aware of it by now.' Ignoring the other occupants of the room, he swept her up in his arms and carried her easily to the fireplace where he gently placed her in the rocking chair that Cook used each evening.

'It cannot have taken, my love. As soon as we have the door open, I'll go and investigate. Remain here; you're not as well as you believe. Leave matters to us.'

She'd had done her part. She would rest as he suggested. Although the blow to her temple was of no account, the headache it had left her with, combined with her fatigue, was making it difficult for her to stay awake. She closed her eyes, letting the sounds of the room drift away. She was roused when Simon knelt down beside her.

'Let me look at your injury.' With gentle hands, he raised her head and with a soft, wet cloth wiped away the blood from her cheek. 'It's not a serious cut. You won't need stitches.'

Whilst she'd been recovering, the

candles had been placed around the room. The men were subdued, no-one was talking much. Suddenly her hands clenched. How could they be sitting around so casually when the very future of the country was at risk?

'Simon, they have the book.'

'They do not, my love. I gave them a fake. David scribbled nonsense in a similar volume. They've escaped with a useless copy.'

Relief almost overwhelmed her. She drew a deep breath to calm her nerves. Wait. Was that smoke? She sniffed again, she was not mistaken. 'Simon, David. Smoke! I can smell smoke.'

'You're right, Lydia.' Simon took command. 'This table is heavy, we can use it as a battering ram. If we do not release the ladies they will perish in the flames.'

A Terrifying Inferno

Lydia positioned herself in the far corner of the room, pressing her back against the wall whilst Simon organised his men.

'We need to get this table swung round so that it's end on to the doors. On my count, we'll smash it forwards.'

It was a great shame the windows in this room had not been replaced when her father had renovated the building. These still had small leaded panes. It would be impossible to knock them out and effect an escape that way. With much grunting and effort, the table was eventually in position. She sniffed the air; the smell of smoke was still not overwhelming. The fire had not reached this part of the house.

'Right. Ready, men one . . . two . . . three. The men ran forward, hurling the heavy piece of furniture at the locked doors. The impact caused the men behind to cannon into those in the front. If the matter had not been so serious, she would have found it funny. They sorted themselves out and prepared to have a second attempt.

On the fourth assault, the door splintered and gave way. As the door swung open, the aroma of smoke was more evident. 'David, escort your sister from the premises immediately. Jenkins and Sam come with me, we must recover the book. Billy and Fred go up and fetch the ladies.' Not waiting to see if his orders would be carried out, he vanished into the passageway.

'David, I'm not leaving without the staff. There's no point in Billy and Fred being sent up to find them; they don't know the inside of the property like I do.'

'I shall go, you have done enough for tonight. Lydia, I insist that you get yourself to safety, leave matters to me.'

She ignored him. 'Billy, we don't know how bad the fire is. Maybe we can put it out. Take Fred and the other two and find the stable hands. Get pails of water and see what you can do between you to douse the flames.' Dodging around her brother, who was attempting to block her passage, she dashed across the passageway and into the back staircase.

She was barely halfway up when she became aware that the hand resting on the wall was hot. The panels were creaking and crackling as if alive.

Simon reached the head of the servants' stairs. The smoke was thick here, not enough to suffocate but sufficient to give him pause. He removed his neckcloth and hastily tied it around his nose and mouth, indicating to his men that they do the same. He wished he'd had the sense to douse his clothes with water before attempting to recover the book. Should he waste precious time and do so now? Jenkins decided the matter for him.

'We'll not get through that lot safely, sir, not unless we're wet.'

'Back to the kitchen. Let's do it, but we must be fast. From the sound of it, the fire has taken a real hold upstairs.'

Fortunately there was sufficient water in the scullery for his purpose. Snatching up a basin, he scooped it in the bucket and tipped it over his head. He did it a second time and ran out, leaving his men to follow when they were ready. He grabbed a blanket from the back of the chair.

Pounding back up the short flight of steps leading to the main part of the house, he stopped at the top. What he heard sent chills down his spine. He'd had dealings with house fires in the past. They were unpredictable, but one thing he did know, when anyone opened a door the rush of fresh air seemed to fan the flames.

The door was too hot to touch. He wrapped a cloth around his hands and gripped the latch. He was about to put his shoulder against it when he hesitated. Should he go through first and leave his men to follow, or would it be safer if they went together? They thundered up behind him.

'Here, take this, Colonel. Drape it over your head. It sounds mighty fierce out there.'

Seconds later, they were all three cocooned in dripping material and ready to brave the fire. He thanked God that Lydia was safely outside and in no danger.

*   *   *

Lydia could find her way through these particular narrow passageways blind-folded, unlike the ones leading to where Simon had been sleeping. She'd been taking this route to the stable yard for many years. She doubted that her brother would have been able to lead them directly to her bedchamber. The smoke was thicker up there and the heat was becoming unbearable.

Arriving at the entrance to her dressing-room, she hammered on the door shouting as she did so. There was

161

no sign of movement, no response. Surely the women were not already overcome by the smoke? David arrived, panting, at her side.

He threw himself at the door and it opened a fraction. Lydia added her weight and together they charged the door, shouting for someone to come and assist them.

'The house is on fire! Get up or you'll perish in the flames! Dorcas, Martha, where are you?'

'If they're all in your sitting-room they won't hear us banging.'

'But I think they would smell the smoke. It's suffocating in here. If they don't come soon we must try and get in another way.'

It was impossible to shift the heavy piece of furniture the women had moved across the entrance. After a few more futile efforts, Lydia said, 'David, let's try the door in one of the guest rooms. Did Simon get the men to block all the entrances up here?'

'No, there was no time. But he did

tell Dorcas to block all the doors. She might have interpreted that as meaning everything on this floor.'

She led the way at a run, not needing the flickering candle to guide her. She turned the last corner and rushed at the door, expecting it to be shut in the same way as the other had been. This door swung open and she tumbled headlong into the dressing-room. David was too close behind her and tripped over her. They wasted valuable seconds while they untangled themselves and scrambled up.

'It will take time to creep in under the bed chamber doors, Lydia.' By this time they were in the wide corridor that led to the main apartments. The guest suites were at the rear of the house, while both her rooms and David's were on either side of the main staircase. David hammered on the parlour door and Lydia shouted for attention. Hurrying footsteps greeted her call and the door was pulled open. There was no need for her to tell Martha the house was on fire. Smoke suddenly billowed up the central staircase, making them all cough.

'Quickly, everyone, we must get out of the house. The main hall is still undamaged. We must exit through the front since the back of the house is already well ablaze.'

Within five minutes Dorcas, Cook, Martha and the four maids were heading for safety. Lydia led the party whilst David chivvied from the rear. He had just guided the last two girls on to the hall tiles when a hideous roar, like an animal in pain, echoed around them. The girls screamed and clutched each other, refusing to budge another inch.

The fire was approaching at a frightening speed. Lydia and Martha frantically drew back the bolts to the front door and lifted the heavy latch but it remained firmly closed. The key. They needed the key as well.

'Dorcas! The front door key!'

The housekeeper clutched her throat and wailed in anguish. 'It's hanging on the hook in my bedroom. I never thought to bring it with me.'

David shoved the screaming girls in front of him toward the drawing-room.

'We must get out through the window in here. Hurry up! There's not a moment to lose. The smoke is getting thicker.'

Lydia abandoned the front door and bundled the remaining women after her brother. She could barely see; they were all coughing and struggling to breathe.

'Help me remove the bar. I fear there's little time left,' David shouted.

'Dorcas, you must all come over here away from the doors. The smoke is less thick on this side of the room.' As Lydia called her instructions she grasped the other end of the heavy bar that held the shutters. Together, she and David removed it and tossed it to one side. This window would push up sufficiently to allow them to scramble through.

'Martha, take the girls through first, then you, Dorcas, and we shall follow.

Run straight to the stable yard. You can shelter in the barn until something better can be arranged.'

With a final jerk David achieved his objective. An icy gust of wind blew in, sending the curtains horizontal. The sill was high and was a considerable drop to the terrace below. He hoisted each woman up, one by one, and lowered her to the ground. As Dorcas reached safety David turned to assist Lydia.

'I can't leave until I know Simon and the others are safe. They went to the library to fetch the book. They had to go through the worst of the flames.'

'I gave my word to him that I would keep you safe. He can look after himself. He would not want you to risk your life.'

She drew breath to protest but he gripped her arms and all but threw her out into the night. She landed painfully on her knees, adding injury to her indignation. She was on her feet and prepared to climb back in when he slammed the window shut again.

* * *

As Simon stepped into the conflagration, the heat seared his skin making him recoil. He waited until Jenkins and Sam were beside him and gestured that they take hold of his coat flaps, if the three of them became separated they would perish.

The fire had increased its ferocity, but believing they were safe gave him the courage to continue. A lesser man might have abandoned the search. No-one would have thought the worse of him, but the lives of hundreds of military personnel might well be saved from the knowledge contained within the covers of the missing book.

In order to reach the library he would have to go out into the vestibule and then take the first corridor on the left. His lungs were burning. If they didn't get into fresh air soon they would all suffocate.

Putting his head down, he trusted his instincts as they all ran for their lives.

He erupted into the vestibule as his beloved whisked into the drawing-room. What was she doing inside? There was no time to consider that now. She could escape through a window in the drawing-room. He must take his chances in the library.

He gulped a few sweet breaths of cleaner air and headed down the passage that led to the room he needed. The walls were red hot, the panelling creaking and groaning as if a living creature.

The library was at the far end of the house. When they reached it he could feel the soles of his boots burning. The fire was travelling beneath the floor-boards, devouring the basements and storerooms. Only the thick carpet was preventing them from being consumed themselves. The smell of burning wool was enough to tell him their time was almost up.

He groped for the door handle and on his third attempt found it. With a desperate heave he threw his shoulder at the door which had already buckled under the heat. It moved an inch. Jenkins and Sam added their weight and the panels, already brittle and smouldering, gave way.

'Get to the French doors, open the shutters and unlock them. Whatever you do, don't open them until I tell you to. When I give you the signal get out fast.'

There was no need for a candle. The room was lit by a rosy glow from the fire raging at the rear of the house. David had put the book away. Simon prayed he would discover it in the same place as the original volume. He ran his hands along the leather covers. The volume he sought was slimmer and shorter than the ones it had been shelved with.

Yes, he had it. He held it up briefly, flicking it open. He pulled aside his singed blanket and rammed the precious object into his inside pocket.

'Now, boys! Open the window now.'

He covered the remaining few yards

in one bound. The roar of the fire pursued him. He was engulfed in flames and tumbled like a fireball out into the night.

Lydia heard David shout. Forgetting her good intentions, she turned and raced toward the terrace that ran along the south side of the house. As she turned the corner she saw her brother racing towards two men who were attempting to put out the sparks on their garments. Then a wall of fire burst from the library doors and within it was a flaming shape.

It was Simon, it could be no other.

A Lost Love

Lydia's scream ripped the night apart. For a second she couldn't move, paralysed by fear as her worst nightmare was being enacted in front of her. Then her feet moved of their own volition and she was racing towards the burning shape.

David was before her and physically restrained her from throwing herself at Simon to try and beat out the flames with her hands. His men had instantly smothered the colonel with two blankets and were rolling him over on the flagstones.

Her heart was pounding, her stomach somersaulting within her. She struggled against her brother and eventually tore herself away. Desperately trying to control her emotions, biting her lip to hold back her sobs, she dropped to her knees beside him.

He was lying face down. It was impossible to discern what damage he'd sustained. The smell of burning and sodden fabric was so strong she gagged.

'Please don't die. I could not bear it if you did.'

A muffled voice replied, 'I should not be best pleased myself. If you will kindly remove yourself I should like to sit up.'

Too stunned to react, she remained with her knees on the edge of the blankets, preventing him from unwinding himself. Someone lifted her away and she glanced over her shoulder to see David grinning down at her.

'He's trapped inside the covers. I believe he's come through the experience unscathed.'

The bundle began to move and a pair of ruined boots appeared, smartly followed by the rest of him. Ignoring the outstretched hands, Simon sprang to his feet shedding burnt material in all directions.

'It's a blooming miracle. I thought

you'd kicked the bucket for sure this time, sir.' Jenkins spoke what Lydia was thinking.

'A trifle singed around the edges, and I shall require new boots, but apart from that, I'm unharmed.'

'Simon, you should not have risked your life to save a book. No-one would have thought the worse of you if it had been incinerated.'

He shook himself rather like a large wet dog before responding.

'But, my dear, not only am I alive and well, but the book is safely in my pocket.' He delved into his waistcoat and removed the volume. He smiled at her. 'See, this, too, is a trifle singed but still quite legible.'

She wanted to fling herself into his arms and tell him how much she loved him, how brave he was, but he might not appreciate her gesture in full view of his men.

'I'm sure that Fred or Billy might have something you can change into, Colonel Westcott.'

The sound of falling masonry inside the house reminded them that they were far too close to the burning building. Shock was making them all lightheaded.

Simon resumed control.

'Everyone, to the stables. There's nothing we can do to save the building. We are in considerable danger where we are.' He took her hand and together they ran pell-mell for the relative safety of the yard.

Once they were a safe distance from the conflagration, he reduced his speed. She gently removed her hand from his. Whatever his men might think of her ignoring convention, Martha would certainly take umbrage.

Her abigail took her duties seriously and was quite prepared to take her mistress to task. As she had been looking after Lydia since she was a babe, it was only to be expected.

'Colonel Wescott, have you considered the possibility that those dreadful men have stolen our horses? I should be

174

very sorry if either of them were taken by those ruffians.'

He shrugged, covering her in debris from his disintegrating jacket.

'No matter. Whatever mounts they've taken will be recovered when Major Dawkins and his troop arrive tomorrow. The villains will not be able to travel in daylight; they'll be too conspicuous. It will be dawn soon and they will have to find somewhere to hole up for the day.'

Her first concern was to get the female staff somewhere more comfortable than the barn. They were in their night garments, having had no time to go back and change. Billy greeted her cheerfully enough considering the dire circumstances.

'I've sent the women upstairs, Miss Peterson, into the men's quarters. It's warm and there's beds enough for all of them to find somewhere to rest.'

'Good man. Which horses did the thieves take?' Simon asked David, who was listening to his sister.

Simon gritted his teeth. He wasn't

used to being ignored. David flapped his hand apologetically and prepared to follow Lydia.

'I asked you a question. It would be courteous to reply before you trot after your sister like a lapdog.'

The young man stumbled over his own feet, shocked by the sharp remark. 'I beg your pardon, Colonel Westcott. They took one of Lord Grayson's carriage horses and five others. Brutus, it appears, kicked up such a fuss they abandoned the attempt to steal him.' He hesitated as if not sure whether to remain or follow Lydia.

'Check on the broodmares. I wish to speak to your sister in private, but first I must find something else to wear.' Billy shifted uncomfortably. What was the matter now?

'I believe you have some garment that might replace this jacket?'

'I do, Colonel, but the ladies are up there now. I didn't think to . . . '

Simon bit back a terse reply. 'In which case I must remain looking like a vagrant recently escaped from a bonfire.' The man's relief was a salutary reminder that, as commander of this small band, it was his responsibility to see to their welfare and not bark at them as if they were recalcitrant recruits. He would do better in future.

'We could all do with a hot drink. Do you have the facilities to make tea or coffee down here?'

'In the tack room, sir, we have a brazier and a kettle. I reckon we can manage to make a brew. We'll have to take turns as there ain't enough cups for all of us.'

'I'll leave you to organise that. What about the two stable hands who remained in hiding here?'

Jenkins and Sam appeared beside him.

'They are checking on the remaining livestock, Colonel. I reckon they will soon smell the smoke and get restless but it's blowing away at the moment.'

'Excellent. Collect all the buckets and get them filled. Also, see if you can discover a couple of ladders. It's best to be prepared. If the wind changes it will blow burning cinders this way and the animals will panic. They need to be moved whilst they are still calm.'

'Here, sir. It ain't much but I reckon it'll fit.' Sam held out an ancient frock coat he'd unearthed from somewhere.

'It will do, thank you.' Simon peeled off the remains of his own jacket, relieved to discover his waistcoat and shirt were relatively undamaged. They reeked of smoke, but then so did everyone who'd been caught in the fire.

His valet held out the fresh garment and he shrugged it on. It was a trifle snug across the shoulders but a considerable improvement. The wind was bitter and he was grateful to have a warmer garment.

'Do you want me to assist Jenkins, sir?'

'Do that, Sam.' He raised his voice. 'Can someone direct me to Miss Peterson?'

'She's round the back, Colonel

Westcott. Walk the length of the yard and turn right, you can't miss it. The building on the left is where the broodmares are stabled.'

'Thank you, Fred. I have no wish to be interrupted, make sure that all the men are aware of that.'

The groom grinned and touched his cap and a ripple of anticipation flowed around the circle of men. They remembered his actions in the kitchen and thought he was seeking out Lydia in order to propose. That was the last thing on his mind.

What he had to say to her might well mean the end of his hopes, but he couldn't let the matter drop. There were things that must be made clear to this young lady if she was to become his wife.

⋆ ⋆ ⋆

Lydia flopped against the half door of the barn where the young stock were stabled. They were unbothered by all the commotion a few hundred yards away and she sighed. At least her beloved horses were unharmed. But how could she run the stud without a home?

Her eyes filled. Bracken Hall was her life. She'd poured all her love into building it up to the prominence it had. Now everything was in ruins.

Footsteps approached and she turned. In the flickering light of her lantern Simon's outline was clear. She swayed toward him but he didn't hold out his arms. He remained apart. Her despair made her more strident than she'd intended.

'Is something wrong? I expected my brother to join me.'

Her criticism was implicit in the comment. Even in the glow of the single lantern it was apparent her remark had not pleased him. How was it possible that she loved this man to distraction but still, at this precise moment, disliked him? From the way he was glaring, he reciprocated her feelings in full measure.

'I sent him to check on the mares. I wish to talk with you alone.'

If he had said this two hours ago, she would have expected him to drop to one knee and make her a formal offer. From his expression, this was not going to happen. Drawing herself to her full height, her eyes blazing, she stared at him, daring him to make a move.

'I believe you are aware that I am an officer. I command a regiment with every expectation of being obeyed. How is it that you, a young woman ten years my junior, flout my every wish?'

'I am not under your command . . . '

'More's the pity.'

This was enough. How dare he speak to her in that offensive tone? What could have possessed her to believe that she wished to be his wife? Being tied to him would be no better than being a common soldier, her every move would be controlled. She would have no independence whatsoever.

'You are neither my father nor my husband and have no jurisdiction over me. I have no intention of remaining here to be berated in this way. Stand aside, Colonel Westcott. I wish to join my brother. This is my home, my estate and here my word is law, not yours.'

She attempted to step around him but he moved to block her path. From the rigidity of his body, she knew he was barely containing his fury. Perhaps it would be wise to remain where she was and endure whatever fury he was going to tip on her head. Hastily she moved back against the barn. He followed her, not stopping until he was a scant arm's length in front of her.

'Miss Peterson, let us get one thing quite clear between us. In the absence of my brother, I am responsible for your well-being. It is not a duty that I relish I can assure you, but I am in control of everything taking place here tonight.'

Her bravado was rapidly dissipating. This man was a virtual stranger. She had placed herself in a different kind of danger by falling in love with him. A broken heart was not easily mended.

'Thank you for making that clear to me, Colonel Wescott. I am, as you have so rightly pointed out, nothing to you but an unpleasant burden. I apologise for causing you extra distress. Now, if you have quite finished scolding me I would like to continue with my duties, the welfare of my staff and my livestock.' Her voice was commendably firm, not reflecting the misery she was feeling at the ruination of her expectations.

'I have not finished. I wish to know why you disobeyed me and accompanied your brother upstairs. Did you think that risking your life was acceptable? Can you not imagine the distress it would have caused your sister if anything had happened to you?'

'I believe, sir, she would have been equally distressed if my brother had perished. I have no wish to bandy words with you. You have made your displeasure more than apparent. I consider myself suitably chastised.'

'Why must you constantly be at odds

with me? I have only your best interests at heart. I thought I made it clear to you earlier . . . '

'What took place between us was nothing but a reaction to the danger we were in. Whatever you might think, I have never given any indication that I wish to be betrothed to you.'

Good grief! What could have possessed her to say such a thing?

'That is fortunate, Miss Peterson, as I was not aware that I had made you an offer.' He stepped aside, allowing her free passage.

She had nothing further to add, indeed could not have spoken even if she wished to. Her throat was clogged with tears. Tonight she had lost something far more valuable than her home.

Her hopes of happiness were in tatters. The man she loved was not who she had thought him to be.

★ ★ ★

Simon watched her stalk into the red-tinged darkness, cursing his terrible handling of the situation. Why had he not taken her in his arms, told her that if anything had happened to her he would have been distraught?

Instead he'd barked at her, told her he felt nothing for her. He'd made a complete mull of things and had no excuse for behaving like a nincompoop.

Although, it was true, his initial intention had been to make sure she understood her position, that she knew he was in command and would not brook any disobedience from anyone, he had calmed down by the time he'd discovered her.

His anger was a natural consequence of his relief that she was unhurt. All he'd wanted to do then was reprimand her for risking her life and explain that there would be chaos if someone didn't have overall control of matters.

What he had done was alienate the woman he loved. He grinned. He might have lost the skirmish but he'd never lost a battle and did not intend to do so now. Somehow he'd put things right between them, however long it took.

★ ★ ★

David was closing the door to the barn which was far enough from the conflagration to be in no danger.

'Is all well in there? The young stock are fine. We have no cause for concern with them so far.'

'They are equally well settled here.' Holding a lantern close to her face, he touched her wet cheeks with his fingers. 'What's wrong, Lydia? If that man has upset you I'll call him out.'

'There's nothing for you to concern yourself with. I'm not weeping. Like you, my eyes are watering from the smoke. No doubt we shall all be suffering the after-effects of tonight for some time.'

He appeared satisfied with her explanation, which was a relief. The last thing she wanted was for her brother to become embroiled in fisticuffs with Simon.

She blinked back fresh tears. She must desist from thinking of him in that way. From now on he would be Colonel Wescott once again.

Swallowing hard, she stepped aside to allow a groom to run past, leading two horses.

'How many more are there to get out, David?'

'There can't be many more to come. They have been moving from the danger area to the home paddock since you left to check the youngsters.'

Pandemonium greeted her in the main yard. Too many boxes were still occupied. She must put aside her misery and help.

Ignoring the clanking of buckets and the sound of the yard pump being worked hard, she raced to the nearest loose-box. Jenkins staggered past with Sam, a ladder resting on their shoulders.

What was going on? Surely it was far

too late to attempt to save the hall? The night sky was red from the ferocity of the blaze.

The colonel strode past, acknowledging the men who were industriously filling buckets.

'Excellent, the wind could veer this way at any time. If it does, we're ready to protect the stables. God willing we can hold the fire until all the horses are safe.' The words were scarcely spoken when the yard was engulfed in choking smoke and burning cinders floated to the cobbles at her feet.

'I Shall Come To No Harm'

Not only was the wind fanning the flames, it was sending sparks and cinders swirling over the stable roof. Two large pieces of debris hit the stable roof and vanished into the tiles.

Lydia could smell the acrid smoke. The remaining horses began to stamp and circle nervously. Thank goodness the buckets and ladders were ready.

'I must get Peg out first; she'll not budge for anyone else,' she called across to David. There were a few panicking horses to deal with, but her priority was her own mare. Her mount was plunging and kicking wildly.

'I suppose there's no point in asking you to leave this to me?'

'No, Colonel Wescott, there isn't. My horse will not come out for anyone else. David and I can move the horses whilst you organise the fire fight.' She'd done it again, issuing orders to him when it should be the other way round.

'I'll leave the animals in your capable hands. I'll get the women out of the loft as it's the first place that will catch if we don't find the cinders quickly.'

He took charge of the yard, he was more than capable of dislodging the cinders that were burning under the tiles. Leaving him to his task, she turned to the loosebox, yanking the bolts back in order to fling open the doors.

'Steady girl, steady. I'm here now. I'm going to take you out of this horrid smoke.' She slipped around her mare's plunging hindquarters and reached her head. She grabbed the trailing end of her head collar and held on, all the time murmuring soft words of reassurance to the frightened animal.

The horse pulled her off her feet twice more before registering her presence. Shivering with terror, the mare finally lowered her head and buried her nose in Lydia's shoulder.

'Good girl. Come along, quickly now, Peg.'

Slowly she turned the animal around, not an easy task in the confined space of a loosebox, and led her out into the darkness.

Smoke was billowing from the roof, but she could not hear the ominous crackle and roar of flames that would indicate that it had taken hold as it had in the house.

Several ladders were leaning against the roof and the men had formed a human chain, transporting buckets of water to the site of the blaze. She did not stop to see if they were succeeding. She dashed past, taking her horse down to the paddock well away from the smoke.

She turned and raced back to remove another horse from the danger zone. She flew past David as he led a plunging carriage horse, but had no time to do more than exchange a worried smile.

'Young Jim has taken the last one,

miss. We have them all out safe and sound, thanks to you and Mr Peterson,' Fred said as he ran an exhausted hand through his hair.

Lydia could barely stand. 'Thank goodness for that.' The ominous crackling of the stable roof drew her attention. 'We have been lucky tonight, Fred. The men have kept the flames damped down just long enough, another five minutes and we might not have saved them all.'

'I reckon we might well lose the roof, miss, but with luck the rain will put it out before it spreads any further.'

She had been unaware she had been working in a steady, drenching downpour.

'Good heavens, I am soaked through,' she said to no-one in particular, and swayed a little as fatigue caught up with her.

A steadying arm slipped around her waist.

'Indeed, my dear, you are. The tack room is undamaged. The fire didn't get a hold on the loft before the rain doused it. Let me assist you there. I wish you had something dry to put on.'

Too tired to argue, she let the colonel guide her back. She noticed the women were gathered there as well, there was nowhere else to go for shelter. The exhausted men were propped against the walls, seemingly unbothered by the freezing rain.

No-one had any dry garments. Everything at the hall had been incinerated and the clothes belonging to the outside workers were ruined by water and smoke.

Martha greeted her, her face almost unrecognisable beneath the smuts.

'The rain's a blessing, miss. Without it, I reckon the stables and the hall would have burnt to the ground.'

Lydia glanced toward her home, astonished to see the sky was no longer lit by orange and that the hideous sound of burning was gone.

Ignoring the rain, after all she was already wet to the bone, she ran back along the path to join her brother and the colonel who were staring at the roof. It was now necessary to have a lantern in order to see.

'Is the fire really out? I can't believe such a fierce blaze could be extinguished so quickly.'

David turned to her, his teeth white in his blackened face.

'It's a miracle. Whilst we were saving the horses, the good Lord was saving our home.'

'Hardly saved. The kitchens and other offices are totally destroyed. And the fire was fierce in the library as well. How can you be so sanguine? We have lost everything we possess. We are all but destitute.'

The colonel smiled down at her and she could not help responding, her former animosity forgotten for the moment. 'I doubt that it's as bad as you fear. The upper floors at the front of the building appear to be undamaged and the main rooms on the ground floor might not be severely burnt.'

'Does that mean we can go inside and retrieve some clothes? We are likely to catch a cold if we remain in wet garments. Good heavens, only a few hours ago you were apparently on your deathbed. I cannot comprehend how you have the strength to remain upright and to be so cheerful.'

All she wanted to do was find somewhere warm and cosy and fall asleep.

'We can't go inside until daylight, it would be far too dangerous. We must make the best of what we have. Billy is making tea and I instructed the others to gather up all the horse blankets that are not in use. A trifle pungent, but in the circumstances I do not believe we can quibble.'

Leaving the two of them to walk around the perimeter of the building, Lydia stumbled back to join the others. The thought of a hot drink and a warm blanket was enough to keep her moving in the right direction.

She was at the archway that led into

the yard when the sound of carriage wheels approaching on the gravel drive made her pause.

She held up her lantern and saw the bobbing lights of at least two vehicles bowling toward her. The night was becoming more extraordinary by the minute. They had few visitors during the daytime at Bracken Hall so to receive them now was incomprehensible.

Too fatigued to greet whoever it might be, she turned and continued her journey to the welcome warmth of the tack room.

'Billy, someone's coming. Could you alert Mr Peterson and the colonel that we have visitors arriving? I really cannot deal with anything else tonight.'

Martha clucked around her like a worried hen over a lost chick. Lydia was enveloped in a thick horse blanket and gently led to a stool near to the glowing brazier. A hot mug was placed in her fist and she took several delicious mouthfuls.

Nothing had ever tasted so good as that over-stewed, over-sweet tea. She drained it to the last drop and then slumped back against the wall, closed her eyes and was asleep in seconds.

* * *

See? Up there, the windows are not broken and there's no smoke coming from that part of the roof. I think it might be possible to find some usable accommodation when it's light. Your problem, David, is going to be that you have no kitchen.'

'I shall be inordinately grateful if I have anything at all. There's a suitable fireplace in the breakfast parlour. I'm sure Cook will manage with that until we can rebuild.' He paused, tilting his head to one side. 'I can hear someone coming. I hope there's not further bad news.'

Simon hurried to meet the person who was running toward them. Billy burst around the corner.

'Sir, Miss Peterson says to tell you there's two carriages arriving.'

For a moment, Simon was mystified, then it was obvious who the occupants of the coaches must be.

'David, I believe some of your neighbours have come to the rescue. At the height of the fire it would have been visible for miles.'

'The Bentleys are no more than three miles away as the crow flies. But the ford will be flooded and it would have taken them far longer to get here. They will have had to make a detour to the bridge.'

The carriages were pulling up by the time Simon got there. He should really let David greet his guests as it was his house, but the young man hung back, giving him no option but to step forward.

The door swung open and a portly gentleman, much muffled in a caped driving coat, descended with remarkable agility for a man of his size.

'What a tragedy! We saw the flames

and I've come to offer my assistance. I must apologise for being so tardy, the roads are all but impassable after all the rain.'

Simon attempted to wipe the worst of the filth off on his jacket before offering his hand.

'You are most welcome, sir. Simon Westcott, brother-in-law to the Petersons, at your service. I take it I am addressing Squire Bentley?'

The older man grasped it and pumped as if drawing water from a well.

'Indeed you are, sir. I've read much about your bravery in the papers. It's an honour to meet you.' He paused to draw breath. 'Miss Peterson, I pray, is unharmed?'

'No-one has been injured. The horses are safe also. However, there is not one amongst us who is not suffering from the elements. The female staff had no time to dress before leaving the premises and the rest of us are soaked to the bone.'

'I have come to transport as many as possible back to my abode. My dear lady wife is at this very moment having a bedchamber prepared for Miss Peterson. The housekeeper has accommodation ready for as many of your staff as you care to send.'

Simon looked to David. 'How many men do you need here to tend to the horses?'

'It would be best to have them all here, Colonel Westcott. They'll soon dry out once the ladies have vacated the tack room. It's not only the stock. I want to get started on the repairs to the roof of the stables as soon as it's light enough.'

Squire Bentley beamed.

'A wise decision, young man. I have room in my carriages for all the ladies and yourselves, gentlemen. It's wretched weather; the sooner I get you back home the better it will be.'

'Thank you, Squire, but I shall not be returning with you. I must oversee what is happening here. I shall fetch my sister and the female staff directly.' The young man hurried away.

Simon had no intention of deserting his post either. Whatever his personal circumstances, it was imperative he was here when Major Dawkins eventually arrived. The sooner the book was transferred, the happier he'd be.

'I must remain behind also, there's more to this matter than you know. If you would care to accompany me whilst I complete my inspection of the damage, I shall tell you what has transpired here.'

★   ★   ★

Lydia peeled her eyes apart and stared blearily at her brother.

'Did you say that Squire Bentley is here with carriages?'

He reached down and pulled her to her feet.

'I did indeed. He's to take you all back with him.'

'But what about you and the colonel?

The men are worn out and soaked as well.'

Martha bustled forward, closely followed by the other female staff.

'Come along, miss. As soon as we get out of here, the others can come in and get dry.'

Of course. Her brain was woolly or she would have worked that out for herself.

Still wrapped in the horse blanket, she followed David through the dripping yard and out to the waiting vehicles. There was no sign of the colonel, which was probably a good thing. She was bound to say something to provoke him and make matters even worse.

Somehow she climbed into the first carriage then Martha, Dorcas and Cook joined her. The remaining girls scrambled into the second vehicle behind Lydia. The door slammed and the coachman snapped his whip. She roused herself from her lethargy.

'Wait! We must take three of the men

as well. Lord Grayson's coachman is an elderly man, as are Jethro and Jed. Quickly, Martha, tell the driver to stop. I'm going to fetch them. I should never forgive myself if they caught congestion of the lungs from this experience.'

The coach rocked to a standstill. Fortunately, it had only moved a few yards. Not waiting for the groom to scramble down and lower the steps, Lydia jumped to the ground, her own fatigue temporarily forgotten.

How could David have not considered this? It was not like him to be so thoughtless. Without a lantern to guide her, she ran toward the flickering lights in the stable yard.

She was on the flagstone path when two shapes emerged from the gloom. She ran headlong into the taller of the two, unable to stop herself. The impact sent them both staggering backward. Two iron hard arms shot out to grasp her elbows and the situation was retrieved. She had no need to enquire as to the identity of her saviour.

'Good grief! My dear girl, I thought I was finally safe from your impetuousness. Why are you not in the carriage with the other ladies?'

Recovering her breath, she stared up at him. She expected to see irritation but his expression was more amused than anything else.

'We must take the coachman and Jethro and Jed with us. They are too old to remain here drenched to the bone. I'm sure you can manage without them.'

He had not released her arms. He must do so or Squire Bentley might misconstrue the situation. Her instinct was to topple forward into his embrace. He represented security, safety but she must not give in. He'd made it perfectly plain that he had no time for her, that unless she was prepared to sacrifice her principles and become a submissive wife she would not do for him.

A rush of indignation renewed her strength and she stepped back, tugging her arms from his grip.

One thing was perfectly clear in all the muddle of the past twenty-four hours — it was quite possible to love a gentleman and still have no wish to marry him.

She had no doubt that their love would carry them through the first few months of their relationship, but after that they would be at constant daggers drawn. He would be pushing her to obey his every command and she would be fighting to retain her independence.

'You are right. We should have thought of that for ourselves. Return to the carriage. I'll find the three you've spoken of and send them to you.' He rubbed his eyes and straightened his shoulders. 'Squire Bentley, there's no need for you to remain. We have more than enough men to take care of things.'

'Very well, if you're certain. I have already instructed a dozen men to set out at first light to assist you. They shall also be bringing food and drink. You must be sharp set and your kitchen is totally destroyed.'

Lydia was strangely reluctant to leave. She could see that the colonel was only remaining upright by sheer strength of will. He had been severely wounded scarcely two days ago. She wished he would come with them and get some much deserved rest before returning to take charge of matters here.

His head turned. Their eyes met and something of her worry must have shown in her expression. Instantly, he smiled.

'Go, my dear. I shall come to no harm. I am a veteran and have weathered far worse than this and emerged unscathed.' He pointed to the waiting carriages and she was obliged to comply.

Her legs turned to blancmange. The distance to the chaise seemed an impossible journey. She gritted her teeth. Neither the colonel nor her brother would get any respite and all she had to do was somehow force her recalcitrant limbs to carry her to safety.

Before she could protest, she was lifted from her feet and held close to his heart. He said nothing as he strode towards the carriage. There was no need for words. His actions told her more than any pretty speech could do.

Martha was waiting for her.

'Here, sir. Let me take care of my mistress now.'

'Make sure you do, I hope to find her fully restored when I visit tomorrow.'

Squire Bentley appeared at the door.

'Well, ladies, I hope you will forgive me for joining you.'

'Are the men to travel in the other vehicle, sir?'

'They are, Miss Peterson. Thank goodness you thought of them. They will be well taken care of in my establishment, never fear.'

After a deal of shuffling, room was made for the stout gentleman. Lydia settled back on the squabs, too tired to respond. Why had the colonel said he would be coming to see her? It was all too confusing. She needed a hot bath and a good night's sleep before she thought about the significance of his remark.

A Safe House

Simon remained where he was until the carriages faded into the gloom. He yawned. It was still an hour or two until full light. There was nothing he or any of the men could do before then, so he might as well find himself a dry corner and get some rest. He was about to turn away when a flicker of movement on the drive attracted his attention. At last, it was Dawkins and his men.

'David, alert your staff to the arrival of the troops. They will need somewhere to stable their horses'.

'Are you sure? I can see nothing.' The young man grinned. 'However, I shall bow to your superior eyesight. There's room in the open barn where we put the horses each morning when their boxes are being cleared.'

'They'll not be here for a quarter of an hour — ample time to get organised.' Simon swayed and David grasped his elbow.

'I think you should get some sleep, sir. I can direct Major Dawkins when he arrives.'

'Later. I must speak to Dawkins as soon as he arrives. I intend to ride out with them to catch the traitors but I fear at the moment I am more likely to pitch headfirst into the nearest ditch.' He yawned. 'A hot drink and a few minutes rest will sort me out. Don't look so concerned.'

The young man laughed.

'I cannot let my future brother-in-law risk his neck. Lydia would not take kindly to your demise when she has only just . . . '

Simon was almost too fatigued to clarify the situation. 'You are way off the mark, I'm afraid. Miss Peterson and I have agreed that we do not suit. She requires an overindulgent spouse, to be allowed free rein, to have matters all her own way and that, as you might imagine, would not be possible if she were to become my wife.'

Instead of commiserating, David threw his arm around Simon's shoulders.

'And do you wish to have a meek and subservient partner? You would die from boredom within a month.'

'I do not like to have my instructions ignored. It's in my nature to command. But I have not entirely given up the hope that I might convince your sister that she would be happier with me than on her own.'

'I should think not. Lydia has always been volatile, but she does not hold a grudge.'

Simon could not consider the future until he'd had some rest. His vision was blurred and every bone in his body was protesting. He had a while before he was needed. He trudged through the arch and pushed open the tack room door.

The room was bursting with wet men steaming in the fug created by the closely packed bodies and roaring brazier. He propped himself against the doorjamb for a moment whilst he decided whether to find somewhere else or turn one of the occupants out. It was no longer raining, the wind had dropped and it was several degrees warmer than it had been yesterday.

Jenkins appeared at his side.

'Here, Colonel, put this round your shoulders and perch in the corner before you fall flat on your face.'

★ ★ ★

The jolting stopped and Lydia opened her eyes. Everyone inside was fast asleep apart from herself and Squire Bentley.

'Come, Miss Peterson. Allow me to escort you inside. My dear wife will be awaiting you. Leave these ladies to my staff.'

'Thank you, sir. It's most gracious of you to take us all in. Did I see a help party leaving just now?'

'Indeed you did. A dozen men on

their way to help your brother and Colonel Westcott.'

Every window in the imposing mansion appeared to be ablaze. The front door opened as they approached and Mrs Bentley bustled down the steps, tutting and clucking.

'Oh dear, you poor thing. Come inside at once. I have a hot bath waiting and there will be a tray sent up to you immediately. My girl, Sarah, shall take care of you.'

Lydia caught a glimpse of herself in the mirror as she passed. Her lips twitched. She looked like a scarecrow, and she had quite forgotten she was dressed so inappropriately. It was fortunate she had no time for society, her good name would be gone for good after tonight's escapade.

She scarcely noticed which direction she was led by her hostess until she was ushered into a pretty parlour. Not one, but three girls curtsied to her. The apple-wood fire was a welcome sight. She would like nothing better than to flop on to one of the chintz-covered chairs and warm herself.

'Sarah, take Miss Peterson through and look after her. Jenny, you will assist. Mary, run down and fetch up the tray that Cook's prepared.'

The taller of the three stepped forward. 'If you would care to come this way, miss, we will soon have you warm and dry.

Less than a half hour later, Lydia was comfortably ensconced in bed with a tray across her lap. She thought herself too exhausted to have any interest in food, but devoured everything placed in front of her. The chocolate, warm and thick, was a perfect complement to the freshly baked rolls, strawberry preserve and golden butter.

'I'm finished. Thank you, Jenny. I apologise for causing so much disruption.'

'We're all happy to help, miss. It's a terrible shame to have one's home burnt down around one's ears. Madam says you are to sleep as long as you wish, you will not be disturbed.' The girl pointed to a small bell on the night table. 'If you need anything, please ring and someone will come immediately.'

Lydia drifted off to sleep, wondering what she would wear when she did get up. Mrs Bentley was a head shorter and considerably wider than she. She could not recall if the Bentleys had any daughters of her size. She had no wish to meet the colonel looking anything but her best.

* * *

Simon blinked twice, rubbed his eyes, shrugged off his blanket and was on his way to the exit. He was pleased to note a couple of the men were no longer sleeping. They had returned to work.

It promised to be a fine, bright day, the rain had passed and the frost with it. With luck, the renegades would be rounded up later and he would be free to pursue the irritating, but totally adorable, Miss Peterson.

215

As he stretched and flexed his cramped limbs, a flurry of banging above him attracted his attention. Good. David's men were already repairing the stable roof. He must find the young man. He hadn't yet slept and would be a danger to himself and others if he was scrambling about inside the burnt building later.

Even in the gloom he recognised Dawkins at the head of the approaching troop. He raised his arm and the major saluted.

'Colonel, we saw the fire from miles away. Is everyone accounted for? We would have been here sooner but the wretched state of the roads made that impossible.'

'Welcome, Dawkins. Yes, no-one injured and all the livestock safe. Only the house has suffered real damage.'

Dawkins dropped from the saddle, steadying himself against his horse for a moment. Simon removed the small black book that had caused all this devastation and held it out.

'Westcott, you look like a vagabond. Thank you for protecting this. Your bravery shall not go unnoticed. You must tell Peterson that he will not be out of pocket over this. His home will be fully restored at government expense.'

'Excellent news, Dawkins, but no more than I would expect. Although I look disreputable at present, if you will allow me an hour I shall endeavour to return fully restored and ready to ride at your side.'

'I shall need time to get directions to the most likely places to seek the traitors. Also my men need rest and their mounts must be fed and watered. We should be ready to ride when you return. We shall not leave before full light.'

Simon nodded at David.

'Have you looked inside? I think the front of the house safe enough to enter; the roof is intact on that side. Unfortunately I doubt that Miss Peterson's accommodation is still habitable. Although the roof is not fully burnt there it will have sufficient damage to make everything inside unusable.'

The young man seemed unbothered by this information. 'Lydia will have to go back to London and stay with Ellen She can replace her wardrobe easily enough up there. I shall keep the male staff and ask my brother-in-law to take in the others until Bracken Hall is functioning again.'

'Good man. This is no place for a lady, even one as independent and courageous as your sister. With luck, the men and rations Bentley promised will be here at dawn.'

'I've had the cellar, in which we locked the villains, set up as a kitchen.'

Simon slapped him on the back. He was sharp set and the thought of a change of garments and a hot meal of any sort filled him with delight. Such small pleasures were what kept a soldier on his feet during a difficult campaign.

The front door was hanging open and the sound of shifting furniture greeted him as he bounded up the steps. He would have to approach the apartment through a different route, the passageway that led to the library would be unusable.

'You can get to your rooms this way, Colonel. Follow me,' David said from behind him. They picked their way around the smoke blackened furniture in the drawing-room, through the dining-room and a second smaller parlour and they were outside his chambers. Someone was moving around inside.

'Good morning, Colonel Westcott. I was expecting you. There's warm water and clean clothes waiting.'

'And good morning to you, Sam. You look remarkably well, I hope you have found time to rest.'

His valet grinned. 'I snatched an hour. That'll do me for now.'

'I need to wash, shave and change but cannot ride out before I've eaten.'

It took both buckets of water to remove the soot and other dirt from his person. Eventually, freshly shaved and dressed, Simon was ready to leave. He stared sadly at the ruins of his favourite boots.

'I suppose I should be grateful that those are all I've lost, but they have seen every battle over the past five years. They had become almost a part of me. When I return I shall be going to visit Miss Peterson. Then we can all return to London and recuperate.' His borrowed footwear was a trifle tight, but would serve.

He was ready at the appointed time. Brutus was as eager as he to get off. Jenkins had pointed out to him that Edward's carriage was missing its lead horse. Unless they could find another that would do the job they would be obliged to remain where they were. Still, time enough to worry about such trivia when the traitors were apprehended.

Major Dawkins brought his massive black gelding alongside.

'Westcott, how do you feel about swimming that new horse of yours across the river?

★ ★ ★

The sound of the curtains rattling jerked Lydia from a deep repose. She opened her eyes to see sunlight checkering the floorboards. She pushed herself upright, expecting to see Sarah or one of the other girls in attendance.

'Martha, are you well? You certainly look as fresh and smart as ever.'

'I'm sorry to wake you, Miss Peterson, but Lord Grayson has just arrived and is most anxious to see you.'

Lydia's stomach churned. She could hardly bring herself to ask the question.

'Is Lady Grayson unwell?'

'Bless you no. When the carriage failed to return as expected, he guessed something was amiss and set out at first light to discover for himself what had happened.'

'Did he come on horseback?'

'No, he came in a chaise drawn by a pair of handsome bays.'

'Did Mrs Bentley find me anything suitable to wear, Martha?'

221

'Indeed she did. It's a trifle out-moded but will fit you well enough. I'm afraid you will have to wear your riding boots with it.'

Unfortunately, that was not the only thing Lydia was obliged to wear. She was standing in her chemise when Martha held out a corset. 'Do I have to?'

'Yes, ma'am. The dress will not do up without it.'

When she was ready, Lydia regarded the result in the full length glass.

'It's a pretty colour. Rose is not a favourite of mine, but I quite like this gown.'

Although it was nipped in at the waist, not high under the bosom like all her other gowns, the damask silk emphasised her femininity. The high neck and long sleeves were exactly right for an early spring day.

The overall effect was charming but somewhat marred by the toes of her boots showing beneath the hem.

'Are the others well rested?'

'Yes, and his lordship intends for us all to return with him. They are short staffed at present owing to an epidemic of measles.'

'That's fortunate.' She giggled. 'Well, for us, if not for the staff who are so afflicted.'

The welcome smell of coffee and crisply fried ham, eggs and mushrooms greeted her when she emerged into the parlour. Her stomach gurgled loudly.

'Thank goodness. I'm starving, and it can only be a few hours since I cleared the tray that Mrs Bentley so kindly sent up.'

The Manse was familiar territory once she reached the handsome entrance hall. However, the butler glided forward and escorted her as if she were royalty to the grand drawing-room.

She was announced formally. She'd taken no more than three steps into the room when Edward swung her up in his arms, enveloping her in a bear hug.

'My dear girl, what a dreadful experience for you all. If you're ready, I would like to leave immediately. It's already past midday and will be dark in a few hours. The detour adds almost twenty miles to our journey. Ellen will be waiting anxiously. She was determined to come with me and only by promising to return this evening did I persuade her to remain behind.'

'I have no baggage to bring. I just wish to bid farewell to Mrs Bentley and the squire and I am ready. Is there room in the chaise for Martha?'

'Of course. No doubt she has informed you that I'm only too pleased to employ your staff for a few weeks. The remainder must stay here another night, then the chaise shall return to collect them.'

He was so eager to leave that she could not tell him she was expecting his brother that afternoon.

She loved Simon, that much she was sure of, but she was still uncertain whether they could make a match of it. They were so similar in temperament, both wishing to have their own way, both so fond of giving orders that she wondered if they could hope to reconcile their differences.

She sighed. No, far better to leave with a faint glimmer of hope than to know for certain there was no future for her with him.

A Return To Bracken Hall

The water swirled and roared, transforming a mild-mannered stream to a raging torrent. Simon nodded to the major.

'I take it you have the necessary rope?'

'I never travel without it.'

Dawkins shouted instructions down the line and two soldiers trotted towards him, the first already uncoiling the rope from about his person. The trooper dismounted in order to attach one end to a tree trunk. The other he tied around his mount's neck. Simon had used the same procedure on more than one occasion when forced to cross a river with his men.

He smiled ruefully. His boots were about to be filled with water but with luck the rest of him would remain dry. Once the rope was firmly attached, the trooper kicked his horse and without hesitation the animal jumped into the river. It swam strongly across, head outstretched, and was safely to the other bank.

'That horse has done this before. Having a beast so comfortable in the water is a godsend in situations like this.'

'When I've used this method of securing a safe passage, it has been in water much warmer than this. Let's hope no one takes a ducking.' Simon was well aware that if anyone lost his grip on the rope he would be swept away, most likely to his death.

The soldier hadn't been carried too far from his intended exit. Hopefully this indicated that the current was not as strong as it looked on the surface. They had chosen their crossing place carefully as this method required stout trees opposite each other on both sides of the river.

The second soldier tested the rope then quickly attached a leather strap and buckled it tight. With one arm hooked through this, he kicked his horse into the water. The rope guided the animal and gave the rider much needed support.

'I shall go across next, Westcott, then you follow me. I'm sorry that you are obliged to get wet a second time.'

Simon watched, his eyes narrowed. He was unused to following orders, especially from a man he outranked. It was bad form for the men to see him being treated so casually. But it was too late to rectify matters; this was the major's command. Best to leave things as they were.

Dawkins reached the bank without mishap and Simon urged Brutus toward the water. Only as he pushed his arm through the loop of leather did he realise he had no idea if the gelding was comfortable swimming. He was about to find out. His horse hesitated on the bank, his ears laid back. Simon could feel the muscles bunching beneath him.

'Go on, Brutus, you've nothing to

fear.' He kicked again and tightened his grip. The horse plunged forward. If Simon had not been prepared he would have somersaulted out of the saddle. 'Good lad. I knew you could do it.'

He hung on to the strap. His gelding was swimming strongly toward the far bank. The water was lapping above his knees, but his concentration was solely on reaching the far side safely. He did not see the tree trunk hurtling toward them. He heard the warning shout too late.

Brutus was struck behind the saddle. The impact sent the animal beneath the water and Simon found himself dangling precariously from the leather strap. He swung around and saw his horse being carried away.

'Stay where you are, Colonel. Sergeant Mayhew is right behind you. He'll push you to safety,' Dawkins shouted above the noise of the river.

Sure enough, a strong arm encircled his legs. He gripped the leather with both hands and was carried easily to the far side where the major pulled him ashore. Simon's boots were squelching, but he was scarcely aware of these discomforts.

'I must do what I can for my horse. You ride on, Dawkins. When I recover him I shall find you.' Not waiting for a response, he raced along the riverbank, praying he would be in time to guide his horse to safety.

★   ★   ★

During the tedious journey, Lydia discovered Simon had ridden out with Major Dawkins to apprehend the criminals. This meant he would not have been able to visit her so she was more sanguine about heading to town. No doubt he would return himself when the matter was brought to a satisfactory conclusion.

'Edward, are you quite certain that Major Dawkins is in a position to promise Bracken Hall will be fully restored at no cost to ourselves?'

230

'I do not know for sure, but David seemed convinced of the man's sincerity. Anyway, my dear, if the money is not forthcoming I shall make up any shortfall.'

Her eyes brimmed. He was so kind and so very different from his brother. He patted her hand and she smiled across at him.

'You are the dearest brother anyone could wish for. David and I are a sore trial to you.'

'You are my family, and I your legal guardian.' His expression was rueful as he continued. 'I should have been more involved in your lives. Ellen worries so about you both; it is a precarious way to earn your living running a stud farm.'

'I cannot live at Bracken Hall until it's fully restored. For the first time in many years, I must relinquish control. I cannot imagine what I'm going to do to occupy my time.'

He raised an eyebrow.

'Needlepoint is not an option, I imagine.'

'Neither is making morning calls and inane conversation with total strangers at musical evenings and soirées.'

'Well, my dear girl, at least you are spared that for the moment. Ellen will not be entertaining or attending functions until several weeks after she is delivered. She will be thrilled to have you there when her confinement takes place.'

'I shall spend time with the boys. I love their company and they will need occupation these next few weeks. Ellen will need to rest.'

'The doctors have no fear that there will be a repeat of what happened when the boys were born. You must not fret, I am quite satisfied the outcome will be successful.'

Martha was sleeping soundly in the corner. If her abigail had been awake, such a conversation would have been impossible.

One did not discuss intimate family details in front of even the most loyal retainer. Lydia settled back, letting her mind drift, wondering how she would occupy her time for the next six months.

Even her morning rides in the park could not take place. She had not brought Pegasus with her this time and Edward's stable did not contain a mount he would consider suitable.

By the time they reached Brook Street, it was quite dark. Martha was awake and followed Lydia from the carriage. Her nephews had been allowed to remain downstairs and were waiting in the hall to greet her. They threw themselves at her as she stepped inside.

Arthur hugged her knees.

'Aunt Lydia, we've been so worried. Mama says you're to come to her room immediately.'

How Ellen could have known she would return with Edward was a mystery. Had a groom galloped back with news of the disaster?

'As you can see, boys, I'm unharmed. Unfortunately Bracken Hall has not fared so well.'

George tugged at her skirt.

'Why are you wearing this funny gown? What's happened to your clothes?'

'Enough questions, young man. Kindly allow your aunt to refresh herself before she is obliged to answer you.'

'I shall come to see your mama in a few minutes. Why don't you run along ahead and tell her that I'm coming? You could ask her to order me a refreshing cup of tea as well, if you please, as I expect we have missed dinner.'

Arthur skipped around her.

'You haven't. Mama has told Cook to keep it waiting for you.'

Not to be outdone by his brother George chimed in.

'We had nursery tea ages ago. We . . . '

Edward intervened.

'Enough, boys. You have been given a task, get on with it.'

Happy to have something to do, the children raced up the stairs to inform their mother of her arrival.

'Thank you for coming to fetch me, Edward. I shall see you at dinner.'

Ellen was resting on her day bed, but was delighted to see Lydia.

'News of your catastrophe travelled ahead of you, my love. Edward sent his groom ahead on one of your magnificent horses and he arrived three hours ago. I just knew something was amiss. I was beside myself with worry until I had the news that you were all safe.'

'Do you know, Edward said not a word about having one of his team stolen by the traitors and the interior of his new carriage all but ruined.'

'Of course he did not, he will have been as relieved as I that those he holds most dear emerged unscathed from their encounter with those dreadful men.' She pointed to a small chair that was already drawn up close to her. 'Sit there and tell me all about it. I do wish Simon had returned with you, but there you are. He is a soldier through and through, his duty must always come first with him.'

This was something Lydia had already fathomed for herself. It merely confirmed her fears — a wife would be an irksome burden to a military career.

'Do you think he might resign his commission now that Bonaparte is captured and the war with France is over?'

'I should think it highly unlikely, my love. After all, what else would he do with himself? He has no estate to run, no business interests. He's been an officer for ever. He knows no other life.'

All hope was gone. She would not become a nuisance to him. He would be constantly worrying about her welfare and might put his own life at risk because of her. Her happiness must be sacrificed in order to keep him safe.

Making this decision was the hardest thing she'd ever done. Her heart was breaking, but her beloved family would never know her sorrow.

If Simon were to become a civilian, she would not hesitate to accept his offer. Finally, she understood that love did indeed conquer all. Their relationship would have been a tempestuous one. However, they could both have learnt to compromise, and the union would have been all the stronger for it.

But that could never be.

'I think it a great pity, Ellen, for Simon is an attractive man. He would make someone an excellent husband, but I doubt any young lady would be prepared to follow the drum and traipse from country to country in order to be at his side.' She smiled with false brightness. 'To be married to a man who was for ever abroad would be no marriage at all. I could not contemplate marriage with a gentleman who did not have an estate in this country. I have never had the desire to travel and especially not to far flung places like the colonies.'

'My dear, I'm sorry to hear you say so. I had such high hopes that you and Simon might make a match of it. If you loved him you would not hesitate. I should be happy to follow my darling husband across the globe in order to remain at his side.'

Lydia laughed out loud.

'That's funny, Ellen. It's Edward who follows you from place to place not the other way around.'

The boys burst in to announce that refreshments were being brought up from the kitchen and Cook had promised to send freshly baked scones to accompany the tea.

When Lydia eventually returned to her apartment she was sure her sister had no notion how she felt about Simon. Plans were already in hand for a mantua maker to call the next day in order to make her a new wardrobe.

Ellen had given her sufficient underwear and several gowns that would serve for now. Martha was, at this very moment, adding frills around the hems in order to lengthen them. Unfortunately, the only footwear she presently possessed were her riding boots. Even her sister's soft, indoor slippers were uncomfortably tight.

With luck, the modiste might have something suitable she could wear. The instructions sent to this establishment were to bring any completed garments. It was a common occurrence for fashionable ladies to change their minds when they saw the finished article, thus leaving the seamstress with garments to dispose of.

That night, all thought of such fripperies was forgotten when she was awakened with the news that her sister had begun her travail. It was too soon, the baby was not due for another four weeks.

With a sinking heart, Lydia threw on her borrowed garments and hurried to answer the summons from Edward that she was required immediately in Ellen's bedchamber.

★ ★ ★

The river widened as it curved eastward. Simon could no longer see the head of his horse above the raging waters. He vaulted a gate and squelched through a waterlogged meadow. He had to reach his horse before the river joined a tributary and headed directly for the sea.

He pounded around the bend, stopping in delighted surprise. Trotting toward him was his mount, ears pricked and obviously none the worse for his experience.

'Brutus, you're a marvel! Come here to me. Let me see if the log caused you any serious harm.'

The animal dropped his huge head and slobbered on his shoulder. A quick examination showed a slight graze behind the girth, but nothing that would cause any discomfort when ridden. Simon scrambled back into the saddle and rammed his water-filled boots into the stirrup irons.

'We must find the others, old fellow. A brisk gallop shall warm us both. I want this business over, I have a pressing visit to make this afternoon.'

The gelding cleared several massive

hedges without hesitation, thundering across country in the general direction of the soldiers. Simon reined back as he approached the deserted farm in which David had suggested the gang might hide during daylight hours. It would not do to approach at speed. He must dismount and cover the remaining distance on foot.

There was no sign of the major and his men, but neither should there be. Dawkins knew his business. He would have his riflemen in place before he revealed his presence. Tethering the gelding to a convenient bush he stroked his neck affectionately.

'You must wait here, Brutus. Hopefully I shall not be gone long.'

The horse was restless, tossing his head while attempting to dislodge the reins and follow him. Simon couldn't leave his horse behind. The gelding might blunder into the line of fire and be injured. So far, there was no evidence to suggest Dawkins and his men were even here or that the farmyard was occupied by the traitors.

He unhooked the reins and led the animal forward. He'd not travelled more than twenty-five yards when he stiffened. Someone was ahead, whether friend or foe remained to be seen. His pistols, after their dip in the river, would be useless. Silently he withdrew his sword from the scabbard, patted his horse on the neck and vanished like a wraith into the bushes.

Two men walked, unsuspecting, into his path. He stepped out, knocking one senseless with the hilt of his weapon and placing the blade to the throat of the other.

'I should kill you for gross dereliction of duty. If you were my men I would have you flogged.' The terrified soldier shook his head helplessly, unable to form a suitable reply. 'Pick up your comrade. Major Dawkins will not be happy you were strolling about the countryside with no heed for anything'.

Brutus arrived at his shoulder and

Simon reclaimed the reins. The unfortunate troopers stumbled ahead of him, making enough noise to alert all but those who were not as deaf as a wheelbarrow.

Lieutenant Carruthers greeted his arrival with dismay.

'Colonel Wescott, what has occurred? Were these men ambushed?'

'They were. By me. Fortunately, I discovered them. I heard them coming, along with half the county.'

The two men slunk off to rejoin the other soldiers who were sitting about, obviously waiting for the scouts to return from reconnoitring the isolated buildings, when they should be cleaning their weapons or standing sentry duty. Where was the major? This was not good practice; he'd thought better of this man.

Heavy footsteps alerted him. He turned and stared grim-faced at the major.

'Colonel Westcott, glad to have you with us. I see your horse emerged unscathed from his swim.'

'Dawkins, a word with you in private, if you please.' Simon outranked this man. It was time to stamp his authority on this expedition. He strode to the far side of the clearing where the men could not eavesdrop. 'Major, your command is a shambles. I'm taking over. You have not acquitted yourself well so far.'

Instantly the major sprang to attention and saluted crisply, his former insouciance abandoned.

'I beg your pardon, sir. I shall be happy to serve under you. As the men we seek are inside the building, I saw no necessity to post sentries or to be on our guard out here.'

'Do you know that for a fact? Have you seen the horses? Have your scouts returned to tell you all six men are hiding down there? What were you thinking? Any one of them could have walked in here and murdered half your troop.'

The major coloured and made no

attempt to dispute the criticism, but Simon saw anger in his eyes. This mattered not. They were both professionals. A mistake had been made but not a grievous one. Dawkins was a good soldier, but he'd become complacent. He believed having twenty highly trained men under his command sufficient to capture the six renegades.

'Post sentries. Have your men checked their weapons since they crossed the river? The traitors might be few in number but they are professional ex-soldiers. You can be very sure their powder will not be damp.'

'I shall see to it at once, Colonel Wescott.'

'When that's done, select two men to accompany you and take that book to the Horse Guards. Its safety is more important than the capture of these men.'

Dawkins nodded, saluted and marched, ramrod stiff, to do his bidding. At least the horses were well concealed. Brutus had directed his attention to where they were tethered. All he had to do now was wait until the scouts returned. He would take this opportunity to remove his boots and empty them of river water.

He was just replacing the second boot when Lieutenant Carruthers hurried across, saluting smartly before delivering his message.

'Colonel, sir, the scout has returned. I beg leave to inform you that he reports the farm is occupied. There are not six but a dozen horses stabled in the barn.'

'Send the scout to me, Lieutenant, there are questions I need to ask him.'

'Yes, Colonel. The man's reliable; he's the best we have.'

The soldier seemed little more than a boy, but the lad was intelligent and able to answer without hesitation. As Simon thought, the Bracken Hall mounts were amongst those hidden in the barn.

'Tell me exactly what you saw, did the other horses look hard pressed or were they rested?'

'Now you mention it, sir, them others

were fresh as a daisy. I reckon they'd not been ridden today. There were hay and a fair covering of straw on the ground.'

'You've done well. Return to your post. We shall be moving out shortly.'

'Carruthers, have the men dried their weapons, checked their powder?'

'They have, Colonel. There are four riflemen amongst our number. I trust that will be sufficient.'

'More than enough. We outnumber them three to one. We should have them in custody within the hour.' The young officer opened his mouth to question this and then thought better of it. Simon decided to explain. 'Six of the horses belong to Bracken Hall; the other six are the animals they used to get here. They were on foot when they ambushed Miss Peterson so their mounts had to be stabled somewhere in the vicinity.'

'It's obvious now you've explained it, sir. How do you intend to flush them out?'

'Assemble the men and tell them to

keep hidden. I've no wish to alert our quarry.'

A short while later, he led his borrowed soldiers down to the derelict farm. If they thought it strange that an officer of his rank was happy to slither on his belly through the undergrowth they knew better than to comment. The riflemen were positioned, the horses removed from the barn and the remainder of his troop hid themselves around the house blocking off all the exits.

They were ready. Now was the time to put the rest of his plan into action. He gestured and the two nimblest men began their ascent. When they were positioned above the central chimney, they removed the bundles of twigs from their haversacks.

Simon held his breath; but they managed to strike a light, even balanced precariously as they were. The burning twigs were rammed down the chimney and a large stone placed on top of the pot. All around the farmhouse similar bundles were tossed through broken windows. One was even dropped down the chute that led to the root cellar. It was not his intention to burn down the building but to flush the traitors out. The smoke should be enough to choke them if they remained inside.

He drew his sword and crouched, ready to pounce. It would take time, but he was prepared to wait. If his strategy failed they would storm the building. Within twenty minutes, thick smoke was spiralling from every broken window. If the men didn't come soon they would be burned alive.

Coughing and spluttering, the six men finally staggered out. There was no need to demand that they raise their hands and drop to their knees. They did so automatically. The prisoners were slung facedown across the saddles of their own horses and tied hand and foot. Escape would be impossible.

'Carruthers, assume command. My job is done. Take these prisoners to headquarters. Major Dawkins will be expecting you there. I have pressing business elsewhere.'

The young man saluted smartly.

'It's been an honour to serve under you, Colonel Wescott. I've designated four men to bring the stolen horses. They can follow on to London when you have dismissed them.'

'Thank you. It will be too late for them to make the journey today. Expect them some time tomorrow.' He saluted. 'Good luck, Lieutenant Carruthers. You and your men have done well today. I've not served with better.'

When he reached Bracken Hall, the light was fading. Already part of the stables were back in use, and there were lights flickering in the windows at the front of the hall itself. Jenkins was waiting to greet him.

'You got the thieves, sir. We knew you would. The squire's men are billeted in the loft. The rest of us have moved inside. It's warm and dry enough at the front of the house. I reckon the back will have to be demolished. There's no saving any of it.'

'See that these men are fed and their horses stabled somewhere. We shall be leaving tomorrow. Now, the team is complete we can use Lord Grayson's carriage.'

'That reminds me, Colonel. His lordship arrived earlier and went straight to The Manse to collect Miss Peterson.

'In which case we shall travel directly to Brook Street. I want Billy to bring Miss Peterson's mare. You can ride Brutus and lead your own mount.'

All that remained to do here was to speak to David. He could not depart without having matters clear between them.

★ ★ ★

Lydia hesitated outside her sister's chambers. She could hear voices. Edward was in there. Was this a good sign? The wall sconces were lit, the house was awake. No doubt the attending physician had been summoned. She could not dither here. She must go in and offer her support.

Her knock was so soft it got no response. She rapped again and footsteps approached the door. A stranger curtsied and stepped back to allow her to enter. Who was this woman neatly dressed in crisp grey cotton?

'My dear girl, do not look so terrified. Everything is as it should be. This is the midwife, Bletchley, she will not be needed for a good while yet.' Her brother-in-law smiled reassuringly.

'Edward, how can you be so sanguine? The baby is not due for several weeks, surely there is greater risk attached to a premature delivery?'

'Ellen was not exactly sure about her dates. You must not worry, Lydia. I asked you to come down in order to reassure you that this is not like the last time.'

He took her arm and guided her through the sitting-room and into the bedchamber. Ellen rushed across to

252

hug her. 'I told Edward not to rouse you, that you would be distressed, but he would insist and so here you are.'

'Ellen, why are you not in bed? I did not expect to see you running about the place like this.'

Her sister's laugh lifted her spirits. 'Darling girl, it shall be hours yet before I am confined to bed. Doctor Oxford is a great believer in staying active during the early stages of delivery. I feel perfectly well.'

This was very perplexing. 'Then how do you know it is your time?'

'Come and sit down, my love, and I shall explain everything to you.'

It was decidedly odd to be sitting in the middle of the night, drinking tea and eating plum cake with Edward, Ellen and herself in their night attire but the staff attending them dressed as for a normal workday.

'Doctor Oxford had not yet been summoned; Bletchley did not think it necessary.' After spending two hours with her sister and matters had not progressed, Lydia decided she would return to bed. Obviously things were straightforward, both mother and baby were healthy and she could sleep knowing everything was as it should be.

But she was now wide awake. However hard she tried, she could not settle. Her mind constantly turned to Simon. Despite Edward's assurance that capturing the six men would be routine for a soldier of his calibre, she could not help worrying for his safety.

This was, surely, another reason not to marry a man engaged in such a dangerous profession? She would be constantly on edge, expecting to be told he was fatally injured in some battle or other.

She would get up; there was no point remaining where she was. It would be dawn soon and she would take a walk around the gardens until the boys were awake.

She had agreed with Edward that she would take them to see the menagerie at the Tower that morning. They would have a midday meal at Grillons Hotel; they were famous for their ices.

This would mean the modiste would arrive in her absence. Martha would take her measurements and that would have to suffice. Lydia had little interest in fashion and relied on her maid to keep her looking smart.

There would be ample opportunity to worry about replacing her clothes when Ellen was safely delivered.

★ ★ ★

The excursion with her nephews was a success: the animals fearsome, the Tower impressive and the ravens satisfyingly black. However, the ices eaten at the hotel were what George and Arthur enjoyed the most.

With some trepidation, Lydia returned to Brook Street. All the reassurance in the world could not remove her doubts. Would Ellen be delivered safely by now?

'Look, Aunt Lydia. Uncle Simon has come back in Papa's carriage. Do you think he killed anyone with his sword?'

'Don't be so bloodthirsty, George. I trust that you do not intend to ask him any such thing.'

The little boy grinned. 'Course not, but he can tell us what happened, can't he?'

She was relieved that they appeared to have forgotten about the imminent arrival of a baby brother or sister in the excitement of seeing their uncle. Her pulse had only just returned to its regular beat when their vehicle arrived at the front door.

Allowing the boys to descend first with their nursemaid gave her a few more minutes to compose herself. She deliberately took her time, submitting to Martha's ministrations without comment.

The longer she remained inside, the more likelihood that he would not be in the entrance hall obliging her to speak to him.

The heated exchange in which they had both repudiated any interest in each other was fustian. He was not the sort of gentleman to fall in and out of love like a young boy. Inevitably, he would wish to renew his courtship; he would not give up easily.

Whatever her personal feelings, however much she loved him, she would be doing him a grave disservice if she accepted his offer.

As she climbed the steps, she rehearsed what she would say to him if he did get the opportunity to converse with her in private. She must make it quite clear before she was forced to refuse him, that she had no wish to traipse around the world with no home of her own. That should be sufficient for him to keep his distance.

The children had vanished and the vestibule was silent . . . too silent. A sick dread filled her. Something was wrong.

Gathering her skirts, she raced upstairs and along the passageway to Ellen's apartment. As she raised her hand to knock she saw Edward sitting on the window seat, his head in his hands.

With heavy heart, she approached him.

'Edward, what is wrong?'

He raised his head, his eyes glittering and his cheeks pale. 'My dear, there has been an error made on the part of the physician. Ellen is carrying twins again. There could be complications and I cannot go in to see her.'

'There's no need to worry unnecessarily, Edward. She has been so well all through her term, unlike last time when she was sickly. There will be a happy outcome, I am sure of it.'

'I pray that you are correct. It will be several hours yet before we have any news. Simon has just returned. I shall persuade him to play a game of billiards. It might take my mind off things.'

'That's an excellent notion. Perhaps I shall take the boys to the park to fly their kites. It's a perfect day.'

He stood up and accompanied her to the door of her apartment. 'That reminds me, my dear. Your groom accompanied Simon and has brought your mare with him.'

Lydia waited for him to disappear before hurrying downstairs. Billy could give her news from home. Her nephews had been exhausted by their jaunt. Her suggestion that she take them to the park had been merely a ruse so Edward was not aware she would be alone with her worries all afternoon.

Unfortunately, Billy was not to be found and she didn't like to send a stable boy to search for him. Pegasus was well and pleased to see her mistress and she promised the mare she would borrow a riding habit the next day and take her for a gallop in the park. The house was not somewhere she wished to be at the moment. She spent the remainder of the afternoon wandering around outside.

*   *   *

'Sam, I'm going to see the boys before rejoining Lord Grayson.'

259

'Very well, sir. I believe I saw Miss Peterson heading for the stables a moment ago.'

Simon ignored the comment. The last thing on his mind at the moment was pursuing their relationship. Until Ellen was safely delivered, his own interests must be put to one side. No doubt Lydia would be checking up on her beloved mare and catching up on news from Bracken Hall.

Arthur and George were unaware of the drama unfolding on the floor below their nursery. They were full of their visit to the Tower but mainly talked of the ices they had tasted. He left them contentedly playing with their toy soldiers and promised to return to see them before they retired for the night.

He'd had little to do with children of any age, but spending time with his nephews made him realise how empty his life was. Perhaps it was time to have his own family, purchase an estate and resign his commission. He could hardly credit that in the space of two weeks he was contemplating abandoning the army. Now would be an ideal time. With Napoleon out of the way there would be little necessity for someone like him.

He still had ten weeks' leave, plenty of time to make a decision about his future. He was a man of action. Would he be able to settle to the mundane routine of everyday life on a country estate? He shrugged; he would not worry about it for the moment but concentrate on offering what support and comfort he could to his brother at this worrying time.

Neither of them could settle to a game of billiards and it was soon abandoned. 'Simon, you must speak to Lydia when she returns from the park with the children. I'm sure she would like to know exactly what happened after she returned here.'

'She's not out with the boys. They're in the nursery and my man saw her heading for the stables a good while ago. I'm sure her groom will have given her all the details.'

Edward frowned. 'She should not be on her own. When Ellen was so desperately ill after the boys were born she was devastated. She kept a vigil at her bedside. Short of carrying her from the room there was no way to persuade her to rest. By the time Ellen recovered Lydia was more poorly than her sister.'

'I shall go to her at once ... you know how it is between us? I love her and I believe she feels the same for me. However, we parted on bad terms. I mishandled the matter appallingly. I have many fences to mend before I can tell her how I feel. But I can promise you one thing, I intend to make her my wife.' Simon expected his brother to congratulate him, to at least smile and wish him well.

'I'm afraid that she has made her feelings very clear to Ellen. She will not even consider you as a possible suitor unless you resign your commission. She has no wish to be a soldier's wife, even one as high ranking as yourself.'

Simon's stomach roiled. How could he have got it so wrong? Lydia did not love him. His dreams were over. Misery made him speak harshly.

'I have no intention of being manipulated by anyone, and especially not by a young woman with far too much to say for herself and no idea of the meaning of respect.' He scowled at his brother. 'Forget everything I've said. If your sister is not prepared to take me as I am then that is the end of the matter. I've managed very well without a wife so far. No doubt I can continue quite happily to do so now.'

All thought of going to find Lydia was pushed from his mind. He needed to be on his own, to adjust to having his happiness destroyed. Why had he spoken so forcefully? He'd burnt his bridges, left no room for manoeuvre. By the time he had the opportunity to speak to Lydia in private, it would be too late. She would have been told what he'd said. He was a numbskull; had he not just been considering doing the very thing she wanted him to?

He hesitated in the entrance hall, not sure where to go. Was the library still unusable after the damage done by the traitors? He would go out in the grounds. The sun was almost gone and the wind cold again. No doubt a brisk walk would clear his mind.

A Proposal

It was far colder in the garden than Lydia had expected but she was not prepared to return to the house to collect the cloak Ellen had lent her. Time enough to face reality when she'd regained her composure and come to terms with the loss of both her home and the man she loved.

There was a delightful folly at the far end of the lawn. This would be ideal to shelter in until she was ready to return and offer whatever support and comfort might be needed. The folly was also a peaceful place, somewhere she could pray for her sister and the babies. Tucking herself into the furthest corner of the marble building, she bent her head in reverence.

Her turbulent thoughts would not let her settle and she raised her head. Her eyes widened. She pressed herself into the corner, wishing she was anywhere but here. Standing not one yard from her was Simon, his face etched with concern, his eyes gentle. How could she remain firm in her resolution when he looked at her like that?

'I saw you come in here. I wanted to see that you were all right. I'm sorry if I disturbed your meditation.'

Her throat was clogged and her mouth refused to form the words to answer. Dumbly she shook her head, intending that he leave her. Then her eyes spilled and she was too slow to hide her tears from him. One stride and he was beside her. A strong arm looped under her knees and the other around her shoulders as he lifted her from the floor.

'Sweetheart, please don't cry. Let me comfort you. You should not be alone like this.'

She buried her wet face in his shoulder. She had no resistance left. He was offering her something she could not refuse — his strength and kindness.

He tightened his hold and set off towards the house. She should protest, demand to be put down, but she felt protected, enjoying the notion that someone else was making the decisions for her.

'I thought we'd be better here for the moment. I don't want to take you inside until you're composed.'

Her eyes flew open. Good heavens! They were not at all where she'd expected to be. They were in what looked like a storeroom for abandoned furniture and other oddments. This would not do. She should not have allowed him to march across the garden in full sight of everyone with her in his arms, but this was a breach of etiquette and she would be thoroughly compromised.

She struggled and hammered on his chest. 'Put me down, Simon. We cannot be in such a place alone.'

To her consternation, he laughed. She felt the vibrations beneath her hand.

'Darling girl, however much you fight it, you know as well as I do that we are meant to be together. This is exactly the place to convince you that you cannot live without me.'

Drawing the shreds of her dignity together, she attempted to glare frostily at him. This was somewhat difficult whilst being held firmly in his arms.

'Kindly put me down, sir. This is beyond a joke.'

Still chuckling, he set her on her feet but remained within touching distance. 'My love, I know that you told Ellen you would never marry a serving soldier.'

Words tumbled from her lips.

'I did not mean it, not really. I thought you would be safer without having me to worry about.'

He stared at her as if she was fit for Bedlam. 'Are you telling me that you were prepared to make us both wretched because of such a nonsensical notion?'

How could he treat her sacrifice with

such derision? 'I don't like you, not at all. I believe that we will make each other miserable if we are together. We have never been in each other's company for more than a quarter of an hour without arguing about something.'

His rueful smile melted her irritation like frost beneath the sun. 'Ours will not be a calm and peaceful union like that of Edward and Ellen. But it will be a loving one and never dull.'

'I believe that you are under a misapprehension, Colonel Westcott. Unless I am much mistaken I have not agreed to marry you.'

'How true! And I have not yet asked you to be my wife. That can be soon remedied.'

He dropped to one knee and clutched his chest in a ridiculous fashion. She was hard pressed not to laugh out loud at his antics, not entirely sure if he was serious or jesting. 'Kindly get up, sir. You are making a fool of yourself.'

He did no such thing but persisted in

his tomfoolery. 'Miss Peterson, would you do me the inestimable honour of becoming my wife? Make me the happiest of men, I beg you.'

She was still uncertain if he was play-acting, and did not wish to reply until she was sure his offer was genuine.

'If you do not agree to take me, Miss Peterson, I shall pine away from a broken heart and become a pale shadow.'

'You are ridiculous, sir, and as likely to become a pale anything as I am to eat my best bonnet.'

With one smooth movement he was upright, his expression serious. There was no mistaking the love in his eyes. 'Will you marry me, my darling? I fear I cannot live happily without you. In two short weeks, I have fallen irrevocably in love with you. Finally, I understand why my brother is prepared to indulge your sister. I would do anything for you. I want you to be happy and shall go to Horse Guards and resign my commission immediately.'

She stepped closer and tenderly touched his face. 'I will marry you. I love you absolutely. However, if you are certain I shall be no distraction, that you will be in no danger because of me, then I insist you remain in the military. It's your life and I wish to be part of it, too.'

His roar of delight sent a flock of roosting pigeons spiralling into the sky. 'Then shall I tell Edward we are to be united?'

The mention of Edward's name brought reality crashing down on her. 'We cannot say anything today. It would be quite wrong to celebrate our happiness until ... until ... ' She could not bring herself to speak the words.

'Exactly so. Come, sweetheart, we must go in and be strong for both of them. Whatever happens tonight will not change things between us. I shall not return to my regiment without you at my side.'

With his promise held tightly in her

heart, she took the hand he held out and together they walked back to the house. They were met by Edward, his face grey with fatigue.

'Where have you both been? Ellen . . . Ellen . . . ' He could not continue. Tears ran unchecked down his face.

Without hesitation, Lydia ran forward and threw her arms around him. 'Edward, I'm so sorry. We should have been here.'

He pushed her away, shaking his head in bemusement. 'Sorry? Everything is wonderful, I was overcome by relief and happiness. Ellen and the babies are well. I have two beautiful daughters to complete my family.'

'I thought . . . oh, Edward, I'm so pleased for you both. Two girls. What could be better? Have you told Arthur and George?'

'They were the first to know. A short while ago they were with their mother and sisters. I came to find you. Ellen wishes you to go up as well.'

Lydia was away up the stairs before

he had finished his sentence, leaving her betrothed to slap his brother on the back and no doubt give him their good news as well.

She burst straight into the parlour and ran across to pause at the bedchamber door. It would not do to arrive pell-mell and startle the new arrivals.

She stepped into the room, not sure what to expect. The scene that greeted her filled her heart with joy. Ellen was propped up on a froth of white pillows, the boys cradled beside her. She looked tired but radiant.

'Lydia, where have you been? I knew how worried you must be and wanted you to know immediately that all was well.'

'I'm so pleased, I can't believe how blooming you look. I expected the room to be full of people. Has the doctor gone already?'

'Indeed he has, my dear. In fact, he has been wrong at every point in this confinement. There were no complications and both my daughters are a healthy weight. They shall be brought down from the nursery and you can be introduced.'

Lydia knew the babies would be with their wet nurse. Her sister, like most fashionable ladies, did not feed her babies herself. A warm glow of happiness enveloped her at the thought of being in a similar situation sometime in the future, but she would not hand her baby over to anyone, she would take care of him herself.

The sound of male voices approaching sent the two boys scrambling off the bed to greet their papa and uncle. Whilst they were in the parlour, she took the opportunity to kiss her sister. 'Do you have names for your daughters? I suppose you and Edward had only selected one of each as you were told you were not to produce twins this time.'

'We have decided to name them after our mothers, Charlotte and Isabelle. Do you approve of our choice?'

'I think them perfect. I cannot wait to

see my nieces.' Noisy voices in the parlour indicated she had a few more minutes of privacy with her sister. 'Ellen, I must tell you that Simon and I are to be married. I am to return with him when he leaves in two months.'

'Two months? You cannot replace your wardrobe and do all that must be done in so short a space of time. I cannot leave my chamber for two weeks at least and not go out in public for several weeks after that. How can I organise your wedding when I am incommunicado?'

Lydia had no time to reply as Simon appeared, flanked by the boys and his brother. She sprang from the bed and rushed to his side. His smile brought colour to her cheeks. 'I've told Ellen our good news. Now we have a double reason to celebrate.'

Arthur grabbed her hand, his face split by his smile. 'It's three reasons, Aunt Lydia. One for each of my new sisters and one for you and Uncle Simon.'

Amidst the general excitement of congratulations, the new arrivals were proudly brought in by Nanny and the nurse.

The babies were perfect in every detail. Although small, they were wonderfully healthy, their little faces pink. Lydia and Simon took the boys back to the nursery, leaving their parents to spend time alone with the babies.

An hour later, she and her beloved were able to escape. Simon led her back to the drawing-room where they could be alone. As they were engaged to be married, she thought it permissible to join him on the chaise-longue. She had so much to ask him, so many plans to make she scarcely knew where to begin.

'Simon, I know nothing about the life I shall be leading. In fact . . . '

'Hush, darling, we shall have plenty of time before we are wed to talk about that. I have something far more important to do.'

There was no time to protest before

he drew her into his arms and placed his lips on hers. Shocked, she sat back, certain such activities were only permitted between married couples.

'I love you, Lydia Peterson, and intend to kiss you again.'

And he did.

THE END

We do hope that you have enjoyed reading this large print book.

Did you know that all of our titles are available for purchase?

We publish a wide range of high quality large print books including:
Romances, Mysteries, Classics
General Fiction
Non Fiction and Westerns

Special interest titles available in large print are:
The Little Oxford Dictionary
Music Book, Song Book
Hymn Book, Service Book

Also available from us courtesy of Oxford University Press:
Young Readers' Dictionary
(large print edition)
Young Readers' Thesaurus
(large print edition)

For further information or a free brochure, please contact us at:
Ulverscroft Large Print Books Ltd.,
The Green, Bradgate Road, Anstey,
Leicester, LE7 7FU, England.
Tel: (00 44) 0116 236 4325
Fax: (00 44) 0116 234 0205

Other titles in the
Linford Romance Library:

SHADOWS OF DANGER

Angela Dracup

Diana is uneasy when she has a premonition of an air disaster. But when she meets charismatic widower Louis, she is terrified — for he is the man in her dream. Soon she is in love with Louis, but her fear for his safety becomes acute. It seems the only way she can protect him is to marry a man she does not love. Would Louis ever forgive her for leaving him? Would true love eventually win through?

TO LOVE AGAIN

Chrissie Loveday

It is 1945 and the lives of families have changed. The pain and memories of the war years have left their mark. Lizzie Vale, the carefree girl — once an aspiring journalist — has changed and become a dedicated nurse. She fights to help her patients recover from their terrible injuries and falls in love with Daniel Miles. Could they ever have a future? Injuries and family prejudice present seemingly insuperable obstacles, but Lizzie is a force to be reckoned with.

HEARTS AND CRAFTS

Wendy Kremer

Eduardo Noriega struggles financially with running the family estate in Spain. He's also responsible for the farm, his mother and Maria, a family servant. When some furniture is in need of urgent renovation friends recommend Claire, who travels to Casona de la Esquina from England — despite the expense involved. Her arrival upsets Elena, a neighbour's daughter, who imagined waltzing down the aisle with Eduardo. Claire does her job, uncovers an intriguing family secret . . . and changes everyone's plans, including her own.

LAST MINUTE ROMANCE

Sheila Holroyd

Etta Sanderson has to fly to Turkey unexpectedly to help Kaan Talbot guide a group of tourists around the country. At first Kaan resents her inexperience, but they begin to appreciate each other's abilities. When they discover that some of the tourists are using the trip as a cover for criminal activities, Kaan and Etta work together to frustrate their schemes — but despite this success, is it too soon to think of planning a future together?